THE WOLF
IN YOU

A Novel

MARK HASTINGS

The Wolf In You
by Mark Hastings

Copyright © 2019 by Mark Hastings

ISBN: 978-1-938082-35-1 (Paperback)
        978-1-938082-36-8 (eBook)

Published by:

Zeloo Media
Oldsmar, FL 34677
USA

For Melissa

Prologue:
"The Wolf in Me"

This is the tale of Olivia Hunter... this is the story of how she lived, how she died, and how she was reborn. This is the story of a young woman, from a normal British family, from a normal English town near the South Coast of Great Britain. This is a tale... a story... a memory of a life-forgotten – one which propelled an ordinary young woman into an extraordinary world, which saw this young woman become the vital piece of a puzzle. This is the story of a woman who became a wolf... who sacrificed her identity, her life... and who now, after so long, is returning to the world she knew... and that woman is you, Olivia Hunter. Awaken, Olivia... your daughter is waiting for you!

Who? What? I? They? We? The dark? The light? That sound? Something? A rumble? A drum? A pulse? A heart-beat? I am feeling things... I can see things... flashing before my eyes... dreams? Memories? My parents? Faces... places... voices... that seem familiar... but, I can't remember who they are? I think one of the faces is... I think their name is... Terry? But, I don't know who they are, nor what they mean? It is as if I have buried them and left them behind on a deserted-island after deciding to set-sail across an ocean, and now I am returning and uncovering the treasures and the people that I left behind? I hear wind-chimes... I hear a beautiful melody. An intense flash of light. I... I... I'm opening my eyes... I can see... I can see the face of a beautiful blonde-haired girl. Who? Who is she? I know her? How do I know her? And then, I see something in her eyes, I see something in her face... and I know... I know who she is... I recognize her smile, her eyes – it's like I am staring into a mirror and at my own reflection.

At first, I think I am looking at a picture of myself as a child – however, then I see the beautiful eyes of the blond-haired girl blink, and I realize that I am in fact looking into the eyes of *Melissa... my daughter.*

Instantly, reality floods back to me – as do memories, faces, names – and I realize that I am lying on a bed.

Sunlight is streaming into the room I am in through a nearby window and making Melissa's big blue-eyes shine like two blue marbles. I start to cry. And then, Melissa opens her mouth and she says:

'Good morning, mommy!'

Melissa? I'm... I'm Olivia again! I'm human again! And the Wolf? The Wolf? They're... Oh my god, they're gone! They're gone! The Wolf is gone?

My heart is racing in my chest. Tears are falling down my cheeks and onto the bed. I am *Me* again, I'm *Olivia* – but, I feel like I am missing something... a piece of my heart, a piece of my soul... *the Wolf?* I feel distraught... I feel sad... I feel lost – but then Melissa puts her right-hand on the right-cheek of my face, and she catches my tears and she says:

'Don't cry, mommy! The sun is smiling. I have been waiting for you to come home.'

And then, for the first time in a long time, I feel... I feel found... I feel happy... I feel love – more intensely than I have ever felt in my life. I blink my eyes over-and-over again – trying to make sure that I am not just dreaming all of this. And then, I hear another voice... *Aiyana?*

'Hello, Olivia! Welcome home! We have been waiting for you for a long time!' Aiyana says with a smile, as she looks down at me from above.

'Where? Where am I?' I ask, as I look up and into Aiyana's brown-eyes.

'You're home, Olivia! You are back where it all began! You must have so many questions? And I promise to give you all the answers you need!' Aiyana says with a smile, before she extends her left-hand – as if offering to help me up off of the bed.

Aiyana helped me up until I was sitting up straight on the bed, and then both she and Melissa helped me to my feet. It was after more than a few attempts at trying to stand up and to steady myself, that I finally stood up on my own two feet. And then, with both Aiyana and Melissa's assistance, I was slowly guided away from the bed where I had been laying, and then out of the bedroom – the same room that I remember sleeping in when I was pregnant with Melissa… in the same house… *Tala's house?*

And when I sit down on the same sofa, in the living room, where I woke up on the morning after Tala found me and brought me back to her cottage – all my memories of the past came flooding back, and I knew exactly where I was.

I'm back in England? I'm back home?

I feel weak – and even just walking those few steps from the bedroom to the sofa here in the living-room, I feel unbelievable pain in my legs… in my back… in my neck… and it even hurts to speak. My eyes also seem sensitive to the bright sunlight that filled the cottage.

I'm home – but, how long have I been here? How long was I away? Melissa is now… she's a little-girl – but the last time I saw her she was only a baby? It's so weird not being able to feel the Wolf anymore – they were always there, right behind my eyes… I miss them! I honestly don't feel the same without the Wolf being there! What happened to them? What happened to me? I'm missing time? I have no memory of anything else after I fell asleep in the snow, outside Aiyana's house, in North Dakota – nor anything before the moment when I just woke up in bed?

Aiyana began to start a fire in the fireplace, while Melissa held my right-hand – as we both sat on the sofa looking at each other and smiling at one-another. *Melissa has a look on her face as if all her Christmases had come at-once.* Melissa looked happy to see me – just as happy as I was to see her. Melissa smiled, and I continued to smile also… I am happy – though I cannot shake the overwhelming sense of utter-exhaustion that I am feeling, and also the intense pain that runs all throughout my body.

Aiyana finished starting the fire in the fireplace, and soon the flames were burning wildly. As soon as Aiyana seemed happy with the fire, she turned around to face both Melissa and I again with a smile on her face. I looked at Aiyana, I looked into her eyes – and, for some reason, everything she did, and just the way that she stood in front of the fire, reminded me of Tala as she had appeared to me the first time I saw her in her human-form.

3

'Can I ask you something?' I asked – looking up at Aiyana, as I held Melissa's hands tightly.

'Of course, Olivia! You can ask me anything!' Aiyana replied with a smile, as she stood in front of the fireplace with the flames of the fire burning behind her.

'Who are you?' I asked, as I looked at Aiyana and I tried to analyze her face – because I am beginning to suspect that she is not who I think she is.

'Who do you think I am?' Aiyana replied with a smile.

'Truthfully? In all honesty? And don't think I'm mad or anything, if I am wrong? But… but, for some reason, something in the back of my head is screaming: Tala! Tala!' I said, as a tear fell from my left-eye – and the more that I looked at Aiyana, the more that I saw the face of Tala looking back at me.

Aiyana laughed, and then she started walking back-and-forth in front of the fire with her head down. And then Aiyana stopped and she looked right at me again, still smiling, and she said:

'I am not Tala! But, something… something that you probably ought to know about me, since you asked me who I am, is that I… I may not be Tala… but I am… I am… her daughter. *Tala?* She… she was my mother!' Aiyana replied hesitantly.

'What? You're… you're her daughter? You're Tala's daughter?' I replied with surprise.

Tala's daughter? But, I thought Tala told me that she couldn't have children?

'She may have been my mother, biologically-speaking – but, Tala and I were very different people. And, before you ask, the one who you knew as *"Mingan"* was not my father. My father was an Englishman, actually, who Tala met when she first arrived here. This house, this cottage, was my father's house – it's been in the family for a very long time, from what I know.' Said Aiyana with a smile, as she looked at me intently.

The way Aiyana is staring at me right now makes me think that she is either reading my mind, or she is just trying to read my facial-expressions. I have no idea what my face looks like – I can't remember the last time I actually stopped and looked at my own reflection in a mirror; however, just looking at Melissa, I am certain that it has been longer than even I could ever guess, at this point?

'How old are you?' I asked Aiyana, as I studied her face. *She has to be around 30, I would guess?*

'Would it surprise you, if I told you that I was in fact 52 years-old?' Aiyana replied with a slight nod of the head.

'*What?!? 52?*' I asked with surprise and in a state of shock. 'But… you can't be? You don't look a day over *30?*'

'Well, that is nice of you to say – but, I am indeed 52 years-old. I was born not far from here. And I have spent the last six months, with Melissa's help, preparing for your return. And, of course, finding you after so long! But, I knew as soon as I saw you, in your wolf-form that you were who I thought you were. The last time I saw you, as Olivia, I was 42 years-old. I have been looking for you… *we* have been looking for you, for 10 years!' Said Aiyana, as she looked from me to Melissa and then back at me again.

'10 years? You have been looking for me for 10 years?' I asked – still in a complete state of shock.

'I'm afraid so! It's been 10 years since we returned to the house in North Dakota to look for you. At first, I thought you were dead… I thought that Tala had killed you. I had no idea where you two were going on that morning – but, I knew that Tala wanted to separate you from Melissa, for some reason. She didn't tell me everything, but I guessed that she was going to try and use Melissa for something – and that you being her mother would try and stop Tala from doing anything that might hurt your daughter in any way. However, when we got back to the house – after I left and I hid us, until I thought it may be safe to return – all that I found was her, Tala, lying on the ground… dead, and in her wolf-form! I knew that it wasn't you who had been killed – I could tell my mother from anybody, even as the Wolf!'

'What? What happened to me?' I asked, with tears in my eyes.

Aiyana then fell to her knees at my feet, and she held both Melissa and my hands in hers.

'I don't know! Every year, at the same time of the year, Melissa and I would return to North Dakota. We would go back to the

5

house, hoping that we would find you there waiting for us. But, you never showed up. We searched wolf-sanctuaries. We posted missing-person posters. But, for 10 years, we never found you! And then, six months ago, we found you! Melissa and I were walking, and we were preparing to head back here to England, when we saw you – in fact, it was actually Melissa who saw you first… she recognized immediately that the wolf that we both saw was really you!' Replied Aiyana, as she looked into my tear-filled eyes.

'What was it that you said, Missy?' Aiyana asked, as she looked at Melissa with a wide-eyed expression of joy on her face.

'I said… I said… there she is! There she is! I knew it was you, mommy! And then, you walked over to me and you let me kiss you on the head!' Said Melissa with the most beautiful smile I have ever seen.

'You mean… you mean that I have been… I've been the Wolf, all this time? For 10 years? I was the Wolf – living, breathing, hunting, and killing – in North Dakota, for 10 years? I can't… I can't believe this!'

'I know how you must feel! We are not sure what happened after we left – but, when we returned and I found Tala dead, you were nowhere to be seen. It's a miracle that we found you – especially after so long! I thought the worst for the longest – but, we never gave up hope of finding you again.' Said a tearful Aiyana.

'I don't remember any of it! I don't remember anything from the past 10 years, at all! I can't believe that I was the Wolf for that long and I don't remember a second?' I said, as tears continued to fall from my eyes. 'How? How did you get me to change back?'

'Well, as you can imagine, it took a long time to get you back here to England? Of course, you were still a wolf when we got you back here. And, when we did get you back here, we… we didn't even know if you would be able to change back into your human-form!' Said Aiyana – before she stood up and then started walking away from Melissa and I. Slowly, I followed Aiyana with my eyes, and then with Melissa's assistance I managed to stand up and be guided over to where Aiyana was standing near a cupboard unit, next to the window in the living room.

I watched Aiyana open the doors of the wooden cupboard, and then a second later she pulled out a small leather pouch – the same pouch that I clearly remember Tala holding and showing me when I first came to this cottage, all those years ago.

'What is that? What's in there?' I asked, as I looked at the leather pouch. 'That was your mother's? I remember seeing her with it a long time ago?' I said.

'Yes, this was hers,' replied Aiyana, quietly, as she looked down at the pouch she was holding with both hands. 'And inside it is what I used to bring you back. To be honest, I almost thought that it would kill you if I gave it to you – however, I hoped that it wouldn't!' Said Aiyana, as she turned around to look at me – and she then opened the leather pouch and pulled out the glass-vile from inside it.

'What is it?' I asked with a whisper, completely mesmerized by the glass vile that Aiyana was now holding – just as her mother had done when she too took it out of the same leather-pouch, now 20 years ago. Although, as I inspected the vile more closely I could clearly see that it had been recently opened and that the contents of the vile were now maybe half of what it was.

'This… this is death – but, from the same token, it is also a form of rebirth!' Said Aiyana with an awkward smile, as she raised the glass-vile up to the light and appeared to be inspecting its powdery-contents. 'My mother always said that, if all else failed, this was the way that she wanted to go! What is inside this little glass container is said to be the last remaining ashes of a creature, called a "Soul-eater" – a mythical creature from my mother's… from Tala's tribe. Stories were told of this "Soul-eater", which was said to come to people at the end of their life and take their souls to the world to come. Probably just a scary-story told to children around the campfire at night? But, I know that Tala believed in it… and I know that she went to great-lengths to obtain this!'

'And what was she going to do with it? What did it do to me?' I asked, tentatively – almost afraid to ask.

'I'm not sure! However, I believe that for Tala this was the means for her to commit suicide – if the need ever came? But, for you, since you are standing here right now and talking to me – I believe that my giving it to you was what killed the Wolf who you were, and the spirit of the Wolf that was inside of you. And, for that, I am sorry – but, to me, it was the only way that I could think to bring you back!'

'What? By killing me? The only way to save me was to kill me?' I asked, angrily.

'But, I didn't kill you – because, here you are! You're alive! And you are Olivia again! And you are free of the Wolf, once and for all!'

'You don't know anything, do you? I was the Wolf! The Wolf was me! I didn't ask you to kill the Wolf, did I?' I screamed, as I turned around on the spot and attempted to walk away.

'If I hadn't done what I did – then who knows how much longer you would have been the Wolf? You may never have come back, and Melissa would never have known her mother? Ever since she was born, I have been telling Melissa what I knew about you and showing her countless pictures that I drew of you!' Said Aiyana from behind me.

'And... and I cannot thank you enough for all that you have done for my daughter... and all that you have done for me! But... but, you don't understand! The Wolf and I... we... I lived so long with them inside me! I have been changing into them for as long as I can remember! I was the Wolf! I WAS THE WOLF!' I said through an unending stream of tears.

'I know, Olivia! Believe me, I know! And, you're right – I don't know what you went through with the Wolf. But, having seen my mother... having seen Tala change over the years, when I was growing up – both physically and psychologically – I can only imagine how much of a true-to-life horror-story it has been for you?'

'You could never imagine! Never! And, if it wasn't for your mother... if it wasn't for Tala... then I would not be here right now! She caused all of this!' I said, as I walked even further away from Aiyana and eventually back to the sofa in front of the fireplace.

'Believe me, if I thought that I alone could have stopped her – then I would have done so a long time ago! She hurt a lot of people! Growing up with her wasn't the greatest, I can tell you!' Said Aiyana, as she followed me back to the fireplace. 'I wish there was something I could say. I wish there was a way for me to change the past and stop Tala from doing what she did to you – what other people did to you also?'

'But, you can't! You can't change anything! Nobody can! Nobody can!' I shouted – so loudly that I even made Melissa physically jump.

'It's ok, mommy!' Said Melissa with a reassuring smile, as she sat down next to me again on the sofa and rubbed my left-arm – as if attempting to console me and calm me down.

'Melissa, I think your Mom needs some time alone? She needs to get some more rest?' Said Aiyana, as she laid her right-hand on Melissa's left-shoulder. 'Why don't you and I head to the store and bring back something for lunch, huh?'

'Ok! Do you want anything, mommy?' Asked Melissa, as she rose to her feet and she stood beside me.

'No, I'm fine! I'll be fine! You... you two go out – I'll... I'll be here when you get back.' I replied, as I attempted to wipe all the remaining tears that still lingered in the wells of my eyes. In all honesty, all I wanted to do was break down and cry – but I didn't want Melissa, nor Aiyana, to see me when I did.

'Well, we'll be back soon! Ok, Olivia? You just lay down and take it easy!' I heard Aiyana say, as I watched Melissa walk away from me and over to Aiyana from out of the corner of my eye.

And then, both Aiyana and Melissa turned around and headed out of the front-door. Soon after, I heard the sound of a car starting and then pull-away.

Within a matter of seconds, I could not hold-back my tumultuous emotions any longer – and I broke down in tears again. I fell from the sofa and onto the floor... to my knees... and I cried... and I cried, until there were no more tears left to cry.

•

Being here... being back here, in the same place in the New Forest where it all began for the Wolf and I so long ago – as the sun shines brightly in the sky above me, as I stand with my beautiful daughter by my side – I feel like I have truly come home! As I look around and I take in everything – everything I see looks exactly as I remember it appearing the last time I was here, and the first time I remember waking up here! It's funny how, even after all these years, a place can stay looking the same – while over the same span of time, the people of the place may have changed, their life may have changed, in more ways than could ever be put into words? Take me, for example: I am willing to bet that no one else in all of England has changed more in the past 20 years than me? It's a miracle I am still here, still alive, and able to return here! One thing I realize now, which I did not know when this whole journey/nightmare began, is that change is not only important – but it is also necessary! Change is what keeps the Earth spinning... the sun shining... the rain falling... the heart beating... change is what makes life worth living!

I don't think my life will be as changeable now, as it was. I have a daughter now, who every day is growing faster than I wish she was. I don't know why I am so surprised that Melissa is growing-up so fast – because, to me, she literally grew from being a tiny bundle of cuteness, into a beautiful and smart little-girl who reminds me so much of the girl I was, seemingly within the blink of an eye! When I look at Melissa now, I see so much beauty and so much hope – just looking at her keeps me smiling and optimistic. Aiyana really looked after Melissa while I was away, and I know that Melissa loves her – but, the greatest and the loveliest thing, to me, that Aiyana did was she kept me alive in the mind and in the life of my daughter... and for that I could never repay her more for doing so! Aiyana didn't have to do anything for me, or for Melissa – but she did. Aiyana didn't owe me, nor Melissa anything – but, now it is us who owes her more than words could say.

I am not sure what I am going to do now, nor what is going to happen next? At this point, my life feels brand new and I feel like I have been given a fresh start. I feel like a child again! I feel like I can do anything! I feel like I can go anywhere! I feel happy! And then, as I look around at my beautiful surroundings again, I start to feel sad – as the memory of the Wolf returns, and I remember them, and I silently thank them for giving me so much.

Would I change anything that has happened in my life, if I could? Would I do anything different, if I had the chance? Like most people, my instant internal reaction and thought is:

Of course! Who wouldn't?

But, in retrospect, as I think back over everything that I do remember, I realize that at no point was I ever given the option to go in a different direction? Or ever truly given the chance to make different choices? It wasn't until I had to think about someone else, and I had to act to ensure the safety of someone who I love, that I had the motivation and the instincts that I needed to make a change that would change not only my life… but also the life of another – and, perhaps many more lives to come? I would do absolutely anything for Melissa – she is so special, and she is so precious… and I know that she is going to have the most amazing life – and, in any way that I can, I am going to make sure that she does. I don't want Melissa to ever know, or to ever have to see, the horrors that I have lived and known – and I want to spare her all the pain that I have felt. But, I do want Melissa to live her life! And I want her to be free to make her own choices – whatever they may be? I have so much that I want to tell her when the time is right… I have so much that I want to teach her. But, for now, I just want us to live and to learn from each-other – because, I know that we can both learn a lot from one-another.

I think about Tala – the witch who turned me into a werewolf all those years ago… I think about Mingan – Tala's psychopathic ex-husband… I think about Alex – my now deceased, psychopathic, ex-boyfriend who raped me while he and I were in our wolf-forms, and who is/was Melissa's biological father… and I think about myself – and, as I try to recall everything that happened, I think about everything that happened that I don't recall... and I think about why everything happened the way that it did, and why people did what they did. And, ultimately, I come to the conclusion that everything and everyone is bound by their nature – not to mention forces that cannot easily be fought against, or controlled.

People care so much about appearances – and someone's identity, whatever that may be, means so much to them and is incredibly important to them. Change is the greatest, and the most fundamental, and the most inescapable, force in the universe – and, sometimes, that fact can be hard to handle, especially when it is staring you in the face.

I close my eyes. I feel the warmth of the sun on my skin. I feel the sensation of the breeze through the trees, on my face and on my arms, and I feel like I am in heaven! This place is so special to me – it always has been, and it always will be!

When I was the Wolf, and whenever I returned here, I felt like this was my home and the place where I would choose to stay forever, if given the chance. This place... these trees... the ground beneath my feet... the air I am breathing now – everything about this place still feels like home, and to me there will never be a time when I will not think about this place and what it means to me. I want to come back here as much as I can, and I plan to come back here with Melissa whenever we can.

It is so quiet – there isn't a sound to be heard from anyone, or anything. There is so much beauty all around – but nothing and no one could ever be more beautiful and perfect to me than my daughter, Melissa.

•

Right now doesn't feel like the end of anything – in fact, everything right now feels more like a new beginning! As my thoughts drift-off again – as if being carried away by the cool breeze – I know that the Wolf is still out there, somewhere, in some other form, and I know that wherever I am there will always be a part of Me in the Wolf, and there will always be a part of the Wolf in Me.

Prelude:
"One Year later"

From the journal of Olivia Hunter:

I have been thinking about the Wolf...
I have been dreaming about the Wolf...
I have been having flashbacks of memory from my time when I was the Wolf every day and every night for the past year — so much that it is as if the Wolf is still in me and is still watching from behind my own eyes in the shadows of my mind, and just waiting for the right time to return to the light and once again howl at the moon?

So, it's one year later. One year since I came home... one year since my parents found out that I was still alive and not dead, as they had feared I was... one year since I woke up in my human body and as Olivia for the first time in 10 years — however, it is only now that I realize and I remember some of the things that happened while I was the Wolf and what I did. And one thing I know for sure is this: the Wolf is not dead! The Wolf is still alive, and they cannot die! How do I know? I just know! I can feel them — just as I used to before.

It's that same knowledge you have when you know beyond any shadow of a doubt that you are pregnant and that you have this other soul, this other mind, this other heart, this other person living and breathing and moving around inside of you, just waiting to come out — and that is what it feels like having the Wolf in Me.

I'm not sure if I should tell anyone, or just keep my secret to myself? But, for now, I am going to stay silent and not mention anything to either Melissa or Aiyana. My day to day life now seems so simple in comparison to my old "wild" life when I was turning into the Wolf on a regular basis — and, to be honest, I miss those days! What am I going to do? I don't know.
What is going to happen next? I'm not sure.
What do I want to happen? I... I... I guess I am in two minds: one side of me thinks that the Wolf coming back into my life would be the worst thing ever — but the other side of me, no doubt the Wolf's influence, is saying to me that being the Wolf again is what I need...
because they are who and what I am supposed to be!
Who knows what is going to happen — but one thing will always be true, either way: I will always be a part of the Wolf, and the Wolf will always be a part of me!

-O.H.

Chapter One:
"Olivia"

My name is Olivia Hunter... and I am a woman who is about to take a brand new leap into the unknown. I am on the cusp of starting the next phase of my life – as a mother to her daughter, Melissa... as a teacher... and as a lover of life – and I am also about to take to the road to change my surroundings, in order to fully explore the next stage of my life – among other things – as a... as a... as a werewolf, as well! Yes, I am a werewolf! There, I said it! And that actually felt really good to say, I have to tell you!

So, I am moving... we are moving – Melissa and me – the two and a half hour, one hundred and forty miles, from the place where I have lived for most of my life, near the south coast of England, to the proudly purported and self-advertised "Centre of England".

We are about to start a new life. Why? Well, quite simply, because I saw that the local Primary School in the village where we are moving to had advertised online that they were looking for a qualified Primary School teacher to fill a teaching vacancy that had opened up – to which I subsequently applied to, and then drove all the way to attend my interview in person. It was probably a month later, after not hearing anything back from my interview, that I got a letter from Meridian Primary C of E School informing me that they had decided to accept my application and offer me the teaching position at their school.

I was thrilled when I received that letter – however, I was also nervous about the prospect of moving so far away from the only place that I had ever known... well, for all my "human existence" you could say?

Of course, I had lived in the United States for ten years – but that was when I was the Wolf, and to be honest I still do not remember all of my time when I was the Wolf and trying to survive in North Dakota all alone.

You could say that my return home from my life as a Wolf, and living in the wilds of North America, back to the reality of humanity and home was hard – mostly because I... we... the Wolf in Me, the Wolf who was me... the Wolf who still is me... we had to die in order to break free of the curse that we were put under. It's a long story. It's a long, sad, traumatic story – the story of my life and the Wolf in Me, from beginning to end – but now that a few of years have gone by, and after discovering that the Wolf in Me was not in fact dead after all, as I had feared that they were, and that they are and they always will be alive within me, I can honestly say that I am incredibly happy to still have the Wolf in Me.

I lived as a wolf... I died as a wolf... I was reborn, as was the Wolf in Me. And, now – at this moment in time – I... we were on the cusp of a new and exciting time to be alive – I could feel it. At this point, I just knew that something amazing and life-changing was about to start its rise on the horizon and enlighten my life, and Melissa's life, in ways that we could not have dreamed about five years ago.

And I was beginning to understand another thing for sure: you truly do not realize how much stuff you actually have until you decide to move. I went over to my parents' house the week prior and I completely cleared out my old bedroom – which they had slowly but surely converted into a makeshift storage room filled with all manner of things – and their garage that was also filled with boxes and boxes of stuff from my childhood. Boxes of old clothes... boxes of old CD's... boxes of old VHS video-tapes... boxes of boxes... boxes of old photographs, some of Terry and me.

Terry – my dearly-departed, handsome and amazing, partner who died far too soon... 15 years-ago now. Even after all this time, I still miss him. I wish Terry was still alive and with us. And I know that if he was then he would have been a great father to Melissa – even if he had not been her biological father – and I know that he would still have loved her as if she were his own. Terry was an amazing man. I miss him so much, and I always will.

17

I went to see Terry's parents a few days before, to say goodbye and to tell them that no matter where I am and what I am doing I will never forget Terry and that I will always love him.

The Wolf tells me every day that I will see Terry again, and I believe them – because Terry will always be irreplaceable to me and I could never imagine spending my life with anybody else or loving anybody else like him. To me, Terry will always be my shining star.

Melissa and I were now on our way to our new home – and we were both completely overcome with excitement and enjoying every moment, and every mile of our long car journey. We sang... we daydreamed... we reminisced... we swapped stories about life, about love, about what we want to do and where we want to go.

And within no time at all, we were there: home – that is, we had arrived at our new house, in our new home village, in the middle of the beautiful and green countryside of England – where and when Melissa and I both believe that our lives were going to *"explode in an amazing, phenomenal, magical, and inspiring rainbow of colour that will give us all that we have ever dreamed of having"* – in the words of my daughter.

However, as soon as we reached our new home and we walked through the front door, and we finished helping the movers move all of our stuff into our new house – most of it still in boxes and bags that we had clearly labeled and colour-coded according to room and person – we were greeted with the almost instantaneous realization that: a) there was not one light-bulb in the whole house; b) there was no electricity; c) there was no heating; and d) there was an odd smell that I can only describe as being "inhuman" and "potent". And, spookily, we also found a silver crucifix hanging from the pull-string of the attic door. But, apart from all that we found when we initially began to take in our new surroundings, our new home felt to both Melissa and I like it could be an amazing home once we were properly settled in. Well, to be honest, I was the one who felt more strongly that it could be an amazing home – more so than Melissa, for some reason – and I hoped that it would continue to feel that way, and I hoped that Melissa changed her mind as time went by.

Chapter Two:
"First Day"

My first day of teaching at my new school felt like my first day of school when I was a kid: I was nervous, I was apprehensive, I was eager to make a good impression – and for the most part I did, I think.

Truth be told, the first couple of hours went fast – and I loved every moment of teaching my class of 11-12 year olds, and I hoped that they liked me as much I already liked them.

Then it was break time for teachers and students alike – and that was when the questions about who I was, where I came from, where I used to teach and for how long, started to be asked – however, not before the Head Teacher, a very smiley woman called Brenda Branch, introduced me to the rest of the faculty:

"Everybody! Everybody, may I have your undivided attention... please? Could I just ask you for a few moments of your time?" Asked Brenda, as she looked around the Teachers Staff Room at all the teachers of the school who were either talking to one another or in the process of making themselves a hot-beverage before the school bell rang and both teachers and students had to return to class.

"I'm sure by now that many of you will have noticed that we have a new addition to our faculty – following the recent departure of our previous Sixth Year teacher, Miss Dawn.

"And I wanted to take this opportunity to officially welcome and introduce our new Sixth Year teacher, Olivia Hunter, to our already amazing and talented faculty of teaching excellence at its finest!" Said Brenda to an entranced audience of wide-eyed teachers who unwaveringly all met her gaze and did not take their eyes away from her for the entire time that she was addressing them.

And then Brenda turned her attention and her gaze towards me.

"I'm sure that you will enjoy every moment that you are with us, Miss Hunter. And I am sure that the class of children who you will teach and come to know will value every lesson that you are the teacher of!" Said Brenda with a warm smile, as she stared deep into my eyes – which made me feel a little uncomfortable there for a few seconds, however I just chalked up her longing stare as being a show of genuine pleasantness and enthusiasm… so I did not feel any cause to worry too much.

"Now, I think that I have embarrassed Olivia here for long enough – and I am sure that you will agree that I have taken up more than enough of your valued break time, so I will leave everybody to continue with whatever they are doing before the time comes when we must all return to educating the wonderful children we are blessed to teach!"

Brenda, or "Miss Branch", seemed sweet – but, in all honesty, no matter her niceties and her stating that all the kids of Meridian Primary school were "wonderful" and that we should all feel "blessed to teach", I knew full-well that every school had some students who were, and who will always be, disruptive – to say the least. I mean, some kids are just prone to disruption and distraction, rebelliousness, and downright, well, blatant ruthlessness, because of either their psychological makeup or their home life. And being a university psychology graduate, I also knew why some children acted the way that they did: they were simply acting on their instincts.

After Brenda was noticeably done with her speech, every member of the gathered faculty returned to what they had been doing before they were interrupted – while I just stood where I was, like a lemming, with what I am sure looked like a dorky and uncomfortable smile on my face, just waiting for the bell to ring again so that I could return to class.

I felt more like a student than a teacher.

Then the bell rang again, and I returned to class.

My first day went well. My first day went fast. I had a mountain of work to do – but I was genuinely loving being back in a classroom and teaching again. And I truly did like the school, the students, and the teachers that I got to talk to that first day. I was hopeful that I was really going to like teaching at my new school.

Chapter Three:
"The Wolf"

It's that time again. The Wolf wants out. The Wolf needs to stretch their legs. The Wolf needs to run, to howl, to hunt, and to do all the things that I, Olivia, think about doing from time to time – but what I, Olivia, cannot do. The Wolf is me – so what I am really saying is that I want to be the Wolf again. Just like the seasons must change from one to the next in an endless cycle, so too must I change.

When I was younger, there was a clear, present, and a conscious distinction between the Wolf and Me – but now, there is no such barrier. It's funny how things change over time, as we all experience new things and grow into becoming who we are meant to be. When I was younger, I used to think of the Wolf as a curse – but, after everything that we have been through together, there is no doubt in my mind that the Wolf and Me are meant to be.

I thought the Wolf was dead. I was… I was distraught beyond measure. I was… I was shocked to be human again after ten years. And I was… I was sad – but then, one year after I returned home to my daughter, I discovered, to my utter delight, that they… the Wolf… were still alive and still inside me. And I must admit to feeling happier than I could ever put into words.

So, that night, after school, after dark, and under the shine of a full-moon – standing naked in the forest of Chantry Woods, not far from our new home, as Melissa slept peacefully without a care in the world – there I stood, Olivia Jessica Hunter, and from within me, and for the first time in a long time, here they came: here came the Wolf.

From the instant that I knew that I was the Wolf again, I was so overcome with emotion that I wanted to cry – because I felt complete again… because I felt so unbelievably and indescribably happy… because I was the Wolf, and the Wolf was Me.

I jumped around. I ran through the forest. I stopped, and then I took a long intake of breath so that I could fully take in every one of the infinite number of smells and aromas that I sensed all around me – some of which I recognized, and some that I didn't. And then I lifted my head up to the moon and the stars above, and I howled loud and long into the air. I was in a state of complete and utter ecstasy. I felt free and unbounded. I felt like I could do anything. I didn't know what I was going to do while I was the Wolf – but, selfishly perhaps, I did feel this powerful urge… this powerful instinct to hunt.

Since I first became the Wolf, more than 25 years ago now, I had become an extremely effective hunter – and I had over time honed my instincts at hunting and killing another animal to an art.

As Olivia, I do recognize and I do believe that every living thing has a right to live and should not be killed for no reason – however, as the Wolf, I know and I understand why death is a natural and necessary act of life.

Having lived the life I have lived as the Wolf, for so many years now, I can tell you that sometimes the old saying "kill or be killed" is one of the most accurate descriptions of nature at its wildest.

I'm not proud that I am a killer – but I did what I had to do when I had to do it. Perhaps that is me being simplistic and attempting to justify and normalize the act of killing another living thing? If so, then that is not my intention. But there is no other way that I could be who and what I am supposed to be if I cannot justify, at least to myself, why I do… why I have done what I have done. After all, I have not only killed animals… I have killed people too – but those who I killed deserved to die for what they did, and of that fact I am certain.

I was the Wolf all night long – and I loved every minute of it. It was just before sunrise, the next morning, when I changed back into my human form and I found myself kneeling on the forest floor and naked from head to toe. Fortunately, I had changed back very close to where I had left my backpack of clothing hanging from the branch of a tree shortly before I had changed into the Wolf.

I retrieved my backpack, and as quickly as I could I changed back into my clothes. After I was fully dressed again I reached into my backpack and I took out my mobile phone to check whether I had received any calls and messages while I had been indisposed – however I hadn't received anything at all. When I looked at the time, and I realized that it was 5.30am right now, I knew that I still had sufficient time to get home and clean myself up before Melissa woke up and discovered that I was not there and had not been there all night long.

Even by foot our new home was 15 minutes away at most from where I was – but, I was tired… very tired… and, to be honest, I had no idea how I was going to make it through a full day of school without falling asleep. I knew that I was going to have to call in and tell work that I was sick, or something – because, even though I didn't feel that bad at that moment, I knew that by midday I was going to be asleep at my desk and being woken up by my class of students throwing all manner of things at me to get me to wake up.

I walked home.

And when I reached home, and I opened the front door, I immediately took off my clothes again – until I was only wearing my underwear – and then I took out my phone from my backpack and I called in to work, and I left a message on the school's voicemail service informing them that: *"I have been up all night… sick… and I unfortunately will not be able to make it in to work today. Regrettably, Miss Olivia Hunter."*

Not a complete lie – seeing as I had genuinely been up all night. And then I climbed into bed and I laid under the covers, and as I looked up at the ceiling of my bedroom I sighed and I smiled with both tiredness and contentment – not to mention with relief, with happiness, and with joy also… because I had just come back from being the Wolf again, after so long, and I felt so… it felt so amazing! So enlivening! So incredible! And I could not wait for the next time – because I loved being the Wolf.

Chapter Four:
"Life is good"

I was beginning to become quite fond of our new home. And I also loved being a part of the community and getting to know the parents of the kids I taught. I loved our new house, the village, the surrounding countryside, the sense of contentment, comfort, and tranquility that I felt... and I loved going for long walks over the green fields with Melissa – in other words, I was loving this time in my life because I was literally having the time of my life: as Olivia, and as the Wolf.

To be honest, I think Melissa found it harder to adjust to our new home and our new surroundings than I did – and I believed at the time that she may have been having a troubling time at school; but, because Melissa was just like me when I was at her age, in so many ways, she remained very tight-lipped when it came to opening up about what was going on in her life. I wanted Melissa to have her own space, and her independence – just as I enjoyed having – and I know that sometimes there are things that can only be said at the right time for them to be said, and not before, which was why I did not confront Melissa with any of my concerns. I knew that she had made new friends, and I had seen her constantly texting and messaging people on her phone: Friends? Boyfriends? I wasn't sure. And even though I respected her need for privacy – as she respected mine – I did, however, wish that she would talk to me more about what was going on inside her. But, as I said, she is just like me – and when I was Melissa's age I kept so much to myself that I was constantly being tripped up by half-truths and blatant lies that I told my friends and my family, and all so that I could keep the Wolf within me a secret from everybody.

I was sure that Melissa would talk to me when she thought it was the right time to tell me what she had been keeping to herself – but, to be honest, I just wished that Aiyana was there to talk to her... because maybe if she were then between the two of us we could have gotten Melissa to tell us what was on her mind.

Chapter Five:
"Cars"

I had been having the worst trouble out of my car since we moved to our new home. I had had my Ford Focus for a couple of years by then, and for all that time I hadn't had any problems out of it – however, since moving to our new home it just hadn't ran right. The engine stalled when it was stationary, it seemed to be using more fuel that normal, and the A/C only worked when it felt like it – rather than when it was needed. Now, I am not embarrassed admit that I know next to nothing about cars – I can drive, I can refuel my car quite expertly, and I could check the oil level of an engine, if I had to; but, apart from that, I am clueless about anything else involving my car, or cars in general. I could probably change a tire, maybe? I passed my driving test first time – however, when I passed my test there wasn't as much focus on car maintenance as there is these days.

There was even a funny instant that happened when I passed my test: I was sat in the drivers' seat of my car, with my driving instructor sat to my left in the passenger seat – and just as I was about to pull away, and start the practical part of my driving test, the rear-view mirror decided that that was the perfect time to slide down the windscreen all the way from the bottom to the top. And when the mirror reached the dashboard, my female driving instructor and I both looked at each other and started laughing hysterically. Even to this day I still remember turning to her and saying: *"Do I need that?"* – To which my instructor just smiled and then replied: *"Only if you think you do?"* It's funny, because when that random moment happened with the rear-view mirror, and the hilarity that followed, after that I no longer felt any of the nerves that I felt just before I stepped into the car to begin my drivers' test. It's amazing how great a good laugh can make you feel.

The thing was, I loved my car! I loved it! And I could never imagine parting with it. It had originally been a very generous gift from my parents to me, after I returned home from being the Wolf for 10 years – my disappearance and sudden reappearance I explained to my parents as being a complete psychological break-down that was caused by losing Terry. And also my decision to run-away and become a nun, and then taking a vow of silence – and that was the reason why I had not been in contact with them, or anybody, for 10 years. Of course, everything I told my parents and my friends was a bald-faced lie – but what could I say? *Sorry, I just had to get away and live as a Wolf for 10 years – mainly because I couldn't change back, even if I tried?*

I wanted to tell everybody the truth when I came back home: that I was a werewolf... that I had been changed, tricked, and manipulated by an evil witch of a woman... that I had made a deal with The Wolf to embody them for as long as I needed to... that I had spent 10 years living as a Wolf... that I had been brought back by Aiyana... and so many other things – however, I didn't, I couldn't, I haven't, and I am not planning on doing so unless I have to one day.

But, back to my car: at the time I was definitely considering the idea of either trading it in, or paying whatever I needed to get it fixed, because I knew that our relationship with one-another could not continue as it was.

Chapter Six:
"Book Day"

Book Day. I will never forget that day. Book day was the day when I was planning to meet my favourite author, and to get a couple of my books signed by them. Yes, my favourite author *Vega* was going to be at the *Bookmark* bookstore in Coventry – and I was going to be there bright and early and first in line to get my books signed.

I had been a fan of *Vega's* for years, and I had read each and every volume of their *"Vampire Spirit"* series of books since the first one came out when I was 16: *"The Vampire Messiah"*.

Vega is an amazing writer, and their books are so unbelievably entrancing, thought-provoking, articulate, and beautifully written that you simply do not want to put them down once you have started reading one of them.

At that point, I had read all seven books in the series, over and over again, and I had dreamed of meeting *"Vega"* – as they were known – for years. And that was the time, and that day was the day!

Vega was kind of a recluse, and their identity was such a mystery that nobody even knew if they were a man or a woman – because they had never clearly and definitively settled the question about what sex they were – and they never, NEVER, did book-signings. Never! So, as this signing was their first signing, and perhaps their only book-signing event ever, I knew that I could not say no to this once in a lifetime opportunity to actually meet my favourite author.

I just wished that Terry could have been there with me. I asked Melissa if she wanted to go with me – but she told me that she had already made plans to meet up with some friends. I was disappointed that she didn't want to go with me – but, to be honest, I was not surprised. Melissa had something on her mind, and I just wished that she would have told me what it was.

Chapter Seven:
"Vega"

So, on Book Day, I went to the *Bookmark* bookstore in Coventry, and I waited outside with the other *Vega* fans – aka. *Fangs*. And we waited. We waited. We waited some more. We waited for hours – what seemed like hundreds of us, and each and every one of us clutching one or more copies of one of Vega's books from their *"Vampire Spirit"* series of books – without any word from the bookstore, nor from *Vega* himself.

Finally, after what felt like an entire day of waiting outside the *Bookmark* bookstore, the doors to the main entrance of the bookstore opened and a young man in his late-twenties came out, nervously holding a piece of paper, and he told everybody waiting outside – as he was no doubt only reading whatever had been printed on the piece of paper that he was holding – that:

"Bookmark must regrettably inform everybody here to attend the book-signing that Vega has unfortunately had to cancel their long-awaited and greatly anticipated appearance due to an unavoidable scheduling conflict – and because of this they will be unable to attend today and meet with you all. However, Vega would like each and every one of you to enter the Bookmark bookstore undeterred and enjoy the gift that awaits you all within."

A scheduling conflict? A SCHEDULING CONFLICT? What the...? No way was this a simple scheduling conflict as we are lead to believe. How rude! How incredible! How... how... how Vega! And, to be honest, that is why I am not that surprised that he decided to "cancel" at the last minute. Hurt? Maybe. But, surprised? No, not really! After all, this would have been the only book-signing he... I mean they had ever done.

I had read in some of the online forums how some people believed that Vega was a woman. Maybe it was the way that they wrote with such blood-lust that made me think that they were a man? Maybe it was the way that they wrote the main protagonist,

Marcus – as if they were writing about a real-life person with all the problems that we all have – vampires, werewolves, and normal people alike? I don't know – but there was just something in the voice that Vega used to tell their stories that convinced me early on that they were really a man, not to mention a writer who could do things to me and to others what writers could only dream of doing… especially female fans of their books.

"Philip" – the *Bookmark Store Manager* – apologized again on behalf of Vega, and then he invited us all to enter the store and receive a free signed-copy of Vega's new book *"The Vampire Rebirth"* that was waiting inside for anybody who wanted one.

Each and every one of us Vega fans were all incredibly disappointed that we would not be able to meet Vega in person – however, in the same breath, we were all incredibly excited because of the fact that we were lead to believe that Vega's new book wasn't going to be available to buy until the end of the year, but now it turned out that there were signed-copies waiting for us. It was because of this revelation that we all decided that the gift of a signed-copy of Vega's new book was in fact a happy consolation prize that we would graciously accept with open arms. Make no mistake, each and every one of us wished that we could have at least seen Vega, even if it had just been for an instant – but there was a genuine belief amongst us all that Vega had done all this on purpose in order to wet our appetite, so to speak.

So, we all went in to the *Bookmark* bookstore – and as promised, and as soon as we entered, each of us were handed a signed-copy of Vega's new book *"The Vampire Rebirth"*: which had on its cover the image of the *"Vampire Spirit"* series' protagonist, *Marcus*, rising from the flames of a fire, with his muscular arms outstretched and his bare chest exposed for all to see. I, for one, was already excited – just by looking at the front-cover, even before I read a single word of the story within.

After I got my signed-copy of *"The Vampire Rebirth"*, I decided to take the opportunity to look around the *Bookmark* bookstore some more and see if there were any other books that I might take a fancy to.

29

So I climbed the staircase to the First Floor, where the Science Fiction & Fantasy section of books was located, and then I went from bookshelf to bookshelf in alphabetical order, clockwise around the vast space, filled from floor to ceiling with books, perusing each and every book cover, and the many and varied book titles that caught my eye. Amazing books by amazing authors from Neil Gaiman to Stephen King, from Anne Rice to Vega – and it was as I was admiring a new *Authors' Preferred Edition* of Vega's book *"The Vampire Life"* – the fifth book in their *"Vampire Spirit"* series – when I felt a presence approaching me, and that was when a shadow fell over me. And after I lifted my head, I was startled to see who it was who was standing over me – because I found myself looking into the dark-brown eyes of a tall man, with shoulder-length black-hair, who was dressed from head to toe in black, and who wore a smile that made my heart instantly flutter like that of a butterfly's wings. The Wolf, on the other hand, did not bat an eyelid – and, if anything, retreated further away from the surface of our shared consciousness… as if they were afraid?

I was lost for words. I was more than a little taken a back – actually, make that very taken a back! Why? Because, well… I don't know? Because, I guess… I… I was, I am, greatly attracted to this mystery man who just came out of nowhere. I just couldn't help myself. Yes, I was… I am… I… he… there was just something… something about him that made my heart want to race, and my knees want to go weak. He is so handsome! So mesmerizing! So gorgeous! So beautiful! So *hot* – as the kids say. And to be honest, for a second there, I thought that I might have been daydreaming about *Marcus* – the protagonist from Vega's *"Vampire Spirit"* book-series – because this man looked exactly like how I imagined *Marcus* to look in my minds' eye. It was as if he were literally a dream come true – because he was real, and I knew he was real… and because everything about him, and the Wolf's reaction to him, told me that he was real.

"Hello", he said with a beaming smile of confidence – with both hands clasped behind his back. Now, I was 5'7 in height, and he towered above me – so I guessed at the time that he must be 6'3? 6'7, maybe?

Looking into his eyes was like staring at two solar eclipses happening synchronously above my head.

I was struck for words... struck for thoughts... struck for any understanding or recollection of where I was – it was as if this mysterious man had transported me away somehow and to somewhere the like of which I had only encountered once before, a long time ago, when I was wherever I was when Mingan made me lose consciousness and when I "awoke" within my mind and I was surrounded on all sides by echoes and reflections.

Who was this man? I asked myself.

"I am so happy to see that you are a fan?" Said the mysterious and dreamy man dressed all in black, as he looked down on me with the most entrancing and hypnotizing gaze I had ever seen.

The man in black then looked down at the copy of the book that I was holding, and he had this look on his face that told me that he recognized both the book and its author.

He must be a fellow fan of Vega's? I thought.

"A fan? Me? I? Yes, yes... yes I am! I... I have been... I've been a fan for years! You? Are you a fan too?" I asked with a nervous smile – and with a distinctive stutter in my voice that echoed the internal mindset of unparalleled bewilderment that I was experiencing at that moment.

"You could say that! Some days I am more of a fan than others, I must admit. However, we have a very close association with one-another – so any feelings of bewilderment with one-another do not last long, usually. I have known them for a long time!" Said the man in black with the hypnotic dark-brown eyes.

"Did you? Did you come here for the signing?" I asked, as I looked longingly into his eyes – all the while feeling as if I were in the middle of a dream from which I would soon wake up from. And then I thought to myself: *of course he's here for the signing – why else would he be here? Get it together, Olivia!*

"Yes... yes, I did!" He replied immediately with a smile, and then shifted his gaze from left to right around the room of bookshelves.

"Shame... shame he didn't show up! Would have been nice if they had actually made an appearance – but I'm sure that he...

31

I mean, I'm sure that *they* had their reasons for not doing so?" I replied with a wide-eyed smile of intoxication.

"He?" Said the man in black, with raised eyebrows – as if expressing a look of utter surprise on his face at my supposition of the sex of Vega. "You said *he*?"

"Well, of course I don't know that they are actually a *He*, per se – but the evidence that they are is there to be found within their books, if you know where to look and what to look for?" I said with a smugness in my voice – mostly due in part to the fact that I had figured out Vega's sex years ago when I first began reading their "*Vampire Spirit*" book series. It was obvious – well, at least it was to me.

"Really? I had no idea?" he replied, as if I had astonished him with a revelation of knowledge that he had not considered before.

"You did see it? You did read and hear the voice of the man behind the words?" I asked playfully, as I looked into his eyes and I lost all concept of everything other than the significance of this moment.

"As a man, I would think that the ever-present and recurring imagery of lust and dominance would have been enough of a give-away to expose the sex of the author, and my favourite author I would like to add? Surely?" I asked with a slight tilt of the head to the left and a playful licking of my lips – and with a look in my eyes that I hoped told this mysterious man that I was just playing with him.

"Are you saying that female authors are incapable of conjuring powerful images of lust and dominance?" He replied – with what looked like an expression of amusement.

He's playing with me too? I thought.

"Not at all! There are many female writers and authors who can describe lust and dominance eloquently – but, in my experience, there is no one like Vega who can... there is no one like *him* who can... well, make a man or a woman go weak at the knees with a single sentence describing two people who love each-other to the moon and back and who would walk through the flames of the gates of hell for one another, if they had to!"

I shivered slightly, as if recalling the sensations that I felt when I read each and every one of Vega's phenomenal and evocative stories of *Marcus* – the undying *Vampire King*.

"So, do you come here often?" I asked with a smile, as I looked longingly into his eyes and I became lost for words again.

"Here?" He replied – the very dashing, handsome, and mysterious man in black, wearing a brazen smile on his perfect face.

I nodded – my head nodding up and down like a nodding-dog figurine sitting upon a car's dashboard – and almost giggling to myself like a little girl at how I felt when the man in black stared back at me.

"Never, actually! Of course, I have been to bookstores before – but never this one. But, I have to say that it is a wonderful bookstore with a vast treasure trove of stories – many of which I would hasten to say that I may have read more than once in my lifetime!" He replied with a wide smile and a glint in his eyes.

"What do you do?" I asked without a second thought as to what I was asking.

"As a matter of fact, I write," he replied without hesitation.

"Really? You're a writer? What do you write?" I asked with excitement in my voice.

"Well…" he started to reply – however, he was then interrupted by the sound of his mobile-phone beeping repeatedly in his inside coat pocket.

The man in black looked slightly annoyed as he took out his phone from the left-hand-side inside pocket of his long black coat – however, not taking his eyes away from me for an instant.

"Hello?" He said, as he answered his phone.

I was mesmerized by him – so much so that I did not know what time of the day it was.

"Yes, I know," he said into his phone – his stare still continuing to linger unflinchingly upon me.

"Yes, of course. I can meet them at… well, I'll message you the time and the place shortly. For now, await my response, prepare for my arrival – but do nothing until you hear from me again," said the man in black – after which he then put his phone back inside his coat pocket, he smiled, and then he said:

"I am so sorry – and now I am afraid to say that I must regrettably leave. I have an appointment to meet. However, it was wonderful to meet you!" He said with a smile, as he reached out his right-hand and touched me on my left-forearm. "I hope to see you again, Miss... Miss?"

"Oh! Oh! I'm... um... I'm... I'm... Oh... I'm..." I replied, as if I were attempting to recover the memory of my own identity from somewhere deep within myself – however, categorically failing in my attempt.

"Well, it was truly wonderful to meet you! See you again!" Said the man in black with a timeless and breathtaking smile – before he turned around and he walked away from me, leaving me... well, leaving me completely stunned and motionless, quite frankly. And I remained like that for a long time afterwards: just standing, staring, thinking, and entranced by the memory of the experience that I had just had with the man in black.

At that moment in time, I felt like I had literally been struck by lightning.

Chapter Eight:
"Something Different"

As soon as I got home, and for many hours afterwards the book-signing, *He* was all that I could think about. Every time I accidentally caught my reflection in a mirrored surface, I could see that I looked as happy as I felt on the inside: I was wearing the biggest grin that I had ever seen myself wear – well, the biggest smile that I had worn for a long time – and it was all because of *Him*.

I also felt *different* somehow. *Different* how? Well, don't know precisely – but I could tell that was just *something different* about me. I was happy – not to say that I hadn't been happy recently, or anything... but I just felt... I just felt so overwhelmingly happy, and maybe for the first time since... since... since Terry?

I wondered... I wondered, if I was this happy, was I... was I... could I possibly be... in love? But, how could I be in love? How could anybody just fall in love with someone who they just met? But, do you know what? It happens! It truly happens – because it happened to me when I first met Terry – and I believed that it was happening again.

But, who was that man? I don't even know his name? And, how could I allow myself to fall in love with a total stranger, and someone who I might never see again? How could the Wolf let that happen?

The Wolf was there the whole time – but they didn't do anything. Nothing. In fact, it felt like they actually retreated a little? But why?

I know that you can hear me. I know that you didn't react for a reason – and, in a way, I'm glad that you didn't. But, I don't know... it just seemed abnormal for you? What is it about this man? What was it about this mysterious man that made you turn into a little puppy and roll-over? Do you have the hots for him too? Do you? I asked the Wolf within me.

I was lost in my own little world for a while there, just lying on my bed and thinking about *Him*, talking to the Wolf, talking to myself, I guess, as the James Bond film *"Goldeneye"* played on the T.V. screen in my bedroom – even though I was not paying any attention to it, until I was thrown out of my dream-state by the sound of the front-door slamming shut. I was startled to attention – as were the Wolf's instincts peaked, especially when we heard the thumping sound of someone's footsteps racing up the stairs. I knew instantly that it was Melissa, and I could tell that she was upset for some reason.

As I sat up, looking at the bedroom door, I could sense that Melissa was standing right outside my bedroom – where she stood for a few moments, as if contemplating whether to come in and see if I was awake. However, within no time at all – and before I could get up and let her in – she quickly opened the door of her own bedroom and she slammed it shut behind her.

I knew that Melissa was upset, and even though I wanted her to have her space and her freedom to be whom she wanted to be and I truly wanted to respect her privacy, and no matter how hard I tried to resist the urge, I knew that I could no long just sit idly by while she was in pain. So I got up out of bed, I walked out of my bedroom, and then I knocked twice on Melissa's bedroom door.

"Missy?" I said through the door.

"Go away!" Melissa angrily replied.

"Honey, please! Open the door? Talk to me?"

"No, Mum! Just… just leave me… just leave me alone!"

"Missy, believe me, whatever is going on within you, I can help you! I was a teenage girl once too, you know?"

Silence.

I knocked on Melissa's bedroom door again.

"Missy, open the door! Open it right now! I mean it!"

"Mum, go away! Just let me… just give me… just… just…"

"No, Melissa! No, I won't! You know why? Because you are my daughter! Because you are my responsibility! And because there is nothing that you are going through that I have not already been through in my life, believe me!"

Silence again.

"Ok, Missy… you asked for it: if you don't open this door right now, then I am going to take your phone… I am going to take away the Wi-Fi… and I am going to ground you for the rest of the year – unless you open up this door right now and talk to me!"

"Mum, please! Just leave… please, just leave me alone!"

"I can't! I can't! I need to know what's wrong… and I want my daughter to talk to me and tell me what she is thinking and feeling, like she used to!" I said with tears in my eyes, as I laid the left-side of my head against Melissa's bedroom door.

"Baby, talk to me… please," I said in a hushed tone of voice – as I simultaneously recalled my Mum and Dad having similar conversations with me through a similar poster-covered bedroom door, way back when I was a teenager and not long after I first changed into the Wolf, and almost every time after I changed into the Wolf – which happened regularly, like clockwork, at the same time every month.

Some things do change – but, for the most part, they stay the same. History has a way of repeating itself. I don't remember being as difficult as Melissa was being then when I was her age? Huh, who am I kidding? I was worse! I never listened to my parents either! I had the Wolf at my back constantly wanting to break out of me so that it could howl up to the sky, run through the forest, and be as wild as they could be.

Then, Melissa's door swung open – and when I looked into Melissa's eyes, as she stood naked in the darkness of her unlit room, I saw that she was in pain and shaking from head to toe. Tears were streaming from her eyes like the constant flow of two waterfalls.

I didn't know what to think, what to say, what to feel.

Suddenly, Melissa ran over to me and she threw her arms around me – like she used to when she was younger – and then she whispered into my left-ear:

"It's inside me."

"What?" I whispered; "What's inside you?" I asked nervously.

"Them… You… Us… Me," she whispered, before she cried harder and as her entire body began to shake more violently.

"I don't understand?" I said, as I too began to cry fresh tears.

I could feel the Wolf start to rise within me – however, I resisted them and I tried to subdue them as much as I could.

Not now! Not now!

Then, Melissa broke free of my embrace and she fell to her hands and knees onto her bedroom floor – her whole body convulsing violently.

The Wolf in Me was coming – however, I resisted again.

And then… and then the realization of what was going on and what was happening to Melissa finally dawned on me through the chaos and the horror that I witnessed happening before my eyes.

"NO!" I screamed at the top of my lungs. "NO! NO! NO!"

I went to reach down and steady Melissa – but it was too late, because she… she had already begun to change.

Then, everything – the world around me, the Wolf inside me – went deafeningly silent, as I watched… as I witnessed… as I saw my little girl transform into a Wolf before my eyes.

"No! No! I didn't want this for you!" I cried, as I fell to my knees. "No! Please, God? No!" But, despite my protests, history repeated itself… and Melissa, my beautiful daughter, followed in her mother's footsteps, and she became a Wolf.

"Oh my god, this can't be happening!" I said, as I looked in horror at Melissa in her Wolf-form, as he looked back at me with what looked like tears in her eyes.

Melissa slowly walked over to me, she put her nose to mine, she opened her mouth to expose a full set of sharp teeth – and then she… she…and then she said:

"Hello… hello Olivia" – to which I did not reply, mostly because, quite frankly, I was in a state of shock: largely because I was starting to realize that where I was and what I saw might not in fact be happening… because I was beginning to belief that I was in fact dreaming. And the person who I was looking into the face of was not my daughter as a wolf – it was *The Wolf.*

"You?" I said silently, nervously. "You? You're not… you're not Melissa?" I asked, as I stared The Wolf in the eye.

"No, I am not – however, I am within her… just as I am within you," said The Wolf – their voice sounded old, wise, and their accent was distinctive, British, like the voice of my favorite actor Judi Dench.

"Why have you come to me now? Why did you show me... show me Melissa changing... changing into a Wolf? Into you?" I asked, as more tears fell from my eyes.

"I am always within you – however, sometimes there are things that must be seen to be believed and understood. And though this is not reality, and you are not awake in the physical sense of the word, this is no mere dream: this is a premonition of what will happen. Your daughter has reached the equinox of her existence, and from this day forwards she will begin experiencing more than she could ever believe to be possible!" Said The Wolf in the always eloquently-sounding voice of Judi Dench.

"I don't understand?" I replied, as I tried to get my head around everything that was happening and everything that The Wolf had just told me.

"Don't worry, Olivia! When the time is right you will know what to do. But, in the mean-time, I must warn you that the path that you are on the cusp of walking down will be wrought with things of a nature that you have not known before. You will meet people, you will do things, you will go to places, and I too will go to those places with you – however, I beg you to be cautious and to not do what you know not to be the right thing to do. Open your heart, yes – but... but do not always allow your heart to dictate your actions," said The Wolf solemnly – their mouth moving in perfect lip-synched synchronicity with that of Judi Dench's distinctive voice.

"I will... I mean, I won't!" I said, as I hesitantly looked away from The Wolf momentarily – before I looked into their blue eyes again, and I said: "I promise, I won't!"

"Well, in that case, I believe that it is time for you to wake up, my child – because tomorrow is now, and now is tomorrow!" Said The Wolf.

I was just about to reply: "what do you mean?" – however, before I could say anything further, I was thrust back to reality and to myself sitting up in bed with sweat pouring down my face, as if I had just awoken from the most terrifying nightmare that I had ever had. It was as I became aware that the bright light of the morning sun was streaming through the open curtains of my bedroom window that I knew for sure that I was truly awake.

Chapter Nine:
"The Morning After"

Breakfast with Melissa and I – the morning after my nightmare – was... it was... it was awkward, to say the least. I just... I just couldn't look her in the eye, because... because I just didn't know what to say. Like I said, it was awkward – and not just for me, but for Melissa also... I could tell. We just sat around the dining-room table, as I ate my butter covered toast a morsel at a time, and as Melissa ate her bowl of cereal one flake at a time while simultaneously holding and looking down at her mobile-phone – both of us in relative silence, only periodically looking up and at one-another for an instant at the most before returning our attention back to our individual breakfast.

This was not how it was supposed to be between us? This was not how it used to be between us not that long ago? What has happened to us? What is going on? And, how is The Wolf involved in all this? In that dream... in that nightmare that I had last night, The Wolf came to me and basically told me that they were also within Melissa – and that one day she too would change into a Wolf just like me. Is that why Melissa has been so withdrawn, secretive, and moody recently? Was I like that when I was her age? I thought – though I already knew the answers to those internal questions.

Why can't we just talk about what is happening? About what is going to happen? Why can't we... why can't Melissa just turn to me, and say: "Mum, I think I'm slowly but surely turning into a werewolf"?

Then it was time for us to part-ways and head to our respective schools – the one where I was a teacher, and the other where Melissa was a student; however, I just couldn't let Melissa out of my sight until I said something to her, just before she left the house.

"I don't know what is going on with you – but I can probably guess how you are feeling right now, because… because I once went through what you are going through. The fear? The uncertainty? The uncontrollable emotions? The burning instincts that you feel rising and getting stronger? The indescribable dreams? The wild thoughts? The voices? Believe me, Missy, if you just talk to me and open up to me about all that you are thinking and feeling on the inside, then I can help you get through it all."

I was almost in tears as I looked into Melissa's eyes.

For a few moments there Melissa said nothing at all – she just looked back at me with this look on her face that told me that she had a lot to say but she didn't know where to start.

After a couple of minutes, Melissa broke her silence and she said:

"Mum, I… I… I know you want to help – but… but what I'm going through… what I am feeling… I… I need to get through alone. But, believe me, if I thought that I couldn't get through it alone then I would come to you. And I know that you would help me. But now is not the time, Mum. Just… just give me time? Please?" Said Melissa quietly with a smile, as she looked at me with a noticeable storm of emotions brewing behind her eyes – and at the same time I could feel something else… some kind of transference of knowledge, over our silent but unbreakable connection, that gave me a reason to feel more confident and optimistic in Melissa's response and her reaction to what was undoubtedly going to happen.

I sensed in Melissa that something may already have happened?

Perhaps… perhaps she had already changed? Maybe… maybe last night, my dream… maybe that was not merely a dream? Maybe… maybe what happened last night actually happened? At least in part? Maybe… maybe I should just trust in Melissa's judgment, and believe that when the time to tell me everything finally arrives she will open up to me unreservedly?

I just kept looking at Melissa and considering all the possibilities – until Melissa turned around, she opened the front-door, and then she left the house without saying another word; however, at that point, I don't think there was anything more that could be said. I just continued to hold out hope that Melissa would one day come back to me.

Chapter Ten:
"Where we're going"

School time always goes by way too slow – whether you are a teacher, or a student – and there is no feeling of elation like that of the moment at the end of the day when the last bell rings out and everybody gets to go home again.

Part of me couldn't wait to leave school and go home – however, at the same time, there was another part of me that wanted to stay sat behind my desk until the morning. Ultimately, however, I decided to do what I knew I needed to do and go home – at least that was my plan, when I walked out of the school office and I made my way across the carpark to my car, until I got into my car and I put the key into the ignition and I tried to start the engine. However, unfortunately, to no avail. I turned the key... I pressed down on the accelerator pedal... I waited... and then I turned the key again... I pressed down on the accelerator again – however, yet again, nothing. It looked as if my car had finally given up the ghost and died – however, leaving me stranded at work with no way of getting home, short of walking... which was what I ultimately decided to do.

I knew that it was only a matter of time before my car decided that it was no longer going to "play ball" – but I just wished that it had done so while it was still parked on the driveway at home, because now I was going to have to pay someone to tow my car home... I was going to have to pay someone to fix it; but, in the meantime, I was going to be without any form of transport for the foreseeable future. *Great huh? My life seemed to be getting better and better and better, right?* I sarcastically thought to myself

Why now? Why does everything bad have to happen all at once? And, why can't I do anything about any of it?

Then I thought to myself: *what the hell am I saying? I don't need a car! I'm a goddamned wolf, aren't I? Well, at least I can be whenever I want to be, right? So, instead of mourning about the death of my car and instead of moaning any further about how bad my life is getting, why don't I just do what I want to do for once, and... and... and be a wolf?*

And then, as if a switch had just been turned on inside of me, I started to run into a nearby patch of parkland that led to a nearby forested area... I dropped my bag to the floor... I took off every piece of clothing that I was wearing... and then, while surrounded by the cloak of darkness that was night, I changed into my wolf-self... and I felt... I felt... I feel unbelievable! I feel indomitable! I feel free! And then I disappeared into the woods, and I knowingly left my belongings behind me.

When I am the Wolf there is no need for words – because nature, in all its forms, speaks to me in more ways that any language could ever hope to.

Having spent 10 years as the Wolf, without change, I am now able to understand and converse with nature at any time of the day or night – even when I am Olivia, in my human-form, and especially when I am the Wolf.

My senses and my instincts feel unfiltered and unbounded when I am the Wolf – which is why I love being the Wolf so much, because they allow me to be uninhibited and unburdened by anything.

As I ran through the dark forest at full speed, enjoying every moment, I suddenly felt that same "presence" again... that same feeling of being watched and observed by something, or by someone? *But what? Who? Were they a threat? Were they a fellow predator? Were they a potential prey? No, I can sense that they are... they are... they are definitely a person, but... but they feel like something, someone different, somehow? I can almost see them in my minds-eye so clearly, and then they are gone again: like a shadow, or more like the shadow of a person? But who?*

Then I heard the sound of a phone ringing, and when I pricked my ears up and I concentrated on the sound that I heard for a few seconds I realized that it was my mobile-phone that was ringing – still where I had left it on the ground near the rest of my belongings – which I also left without a care in the world... and it was then that I realized that there could be only one person who would be calling me at this time of night: Melissa.

So, I decided to race back to where I entered the forest – and in no time at all I found my mobile-phone lying on the ground, which had undoubtedly fallen out of my jacket pocket when I took it off, and when I looked at my phone's screen I saw that it was indeed Melissa who had been trying to call me. However, I was unable to answer my phone – because I was the Wolf, and because no mobile-phone manufacturer has yet come up with a way for a member of the canine family to use a phone and receive and make phone calls – well, not to my knowledge anyway? So, I just had to let the phone ring until Melissa finally hung up.

I tried to change back into my human-form, as much as I could – but nothing happened, and I couldn't do anything about it.

Then I received a text message from Melissa – the notification and the preview of which I could clearly see being displayed on my mobile-phone's screen – which read:

"Mum, I don't know where you are – but I need to tell you that I'm going to…"

And that was all that I could read of Melissa's message, because that was all that could be displayed.

She's going to what? I asked myself. *What does she need to tell me? And why now?*

I didn't hesitate any longer, and I didn't give myself any more time to consider any alternative course of action – other than to return home as the Wolf and find out what Melissa's message was all about for myself.

It didn't take me long to get home as the Wolf – a few minutes, if that – and just in time to see Melissa getting into the passenger seat of a car I did not recognize.

Melissa saw me as soon as I was within a few meters of our house – and she did not hesitate to close the passenger-side door of the car that she was getting into as quick as she could… and as soon as she was inside, the driver of the car did not hesitate to immediately start driving away.

What was she doing? Whose car was that? I thought – just before the car that Melissa had just got into started to race towards me at high-speed, and then it hit me hard and sent me flying to the ground.

I was still conscious – however, in considerable pain – as I laid there on the ground... and it was as I began to feel as if I were about to pass-out – when my vision became blurry, my legs began to feel heavy, and I could no longer think cogently anymore – that was when I felt as if I were turning back into my human-form, and that was when I... that was when... that was when I... that was when everything went dark.

●

"Where am I?" I said immediately, as soon as I opened my eyes and I was greeted by a very bright light.

"It's ok!" I heard a woman's voice say. "It's ok, Jane – you're ok!" Said the woman with the short-brown hair, as she finally took the light of what looked like a miniature torch away from my face.

"Jane?" I replied groggily; "Jane? Who the hell is Jane?" I asked, slurring my words, as I began to fidget around on the hospital bed that I found myself lying upon. And then it occurred to me: *Wait a minute, I'm in hospital? How did I get here? What happened? And why does this woman keep calling me "Jane"? My name is... my name is* – and for a few moments there I honestly I could not for the life of me remember my own name.

Where am I? Where's Melissa?

"You took a big blow to the head – but you're gravy right now. You just need to take it easy, ok?" Said the doctor, as she looked me straight in the eye – who had to have been some kind of doctor, because she was wearing a white-coat, a stethoscope, and an identification badge, that read: *Amanda Dial, Hope Hill Hospital.*

"Do you remember your name? Can you tell me who you are?" Asked the doctor.

"I'm? I'm? Where? Where's? Where's Melissa? Where is my daughter?" I asked with agitation in my voice.

"And I will help you to answer all of those questions in a couple of minutes, when I get back, ok?" Said the doctor with a smile – before she turned around on the spot and she walked out of the room.

I must have blacked out? I must have fainted, or something? I must... I must have... maybe that doctor gave me something? I don't know what happened? I don't know what is going on? I don't even know how I got here? But one thing I do know is that I am not staying here a minute longer! I have to get home! I have to find Melissa! I need to make sense of everything that has been happening! I need... I need... I need to leave before something else happens! I thought to myself.

I looked around to see if anybody else was in my room with me – and when I realized that I was the only person in the room, I wasted no time in pulling open the bed covers of my hospital bed to reveal my bare legs and the blue and white hospital gown that I was wearing. And then I realized that when I turned back into my human-form I must not have been wearing any clothes – which of course meant that when I was brought into this hospital I did so without any kind of belongings at all, nor without any form identification.

That probably explains why that doctor called me "Jane" when I woke up. "Jane" for "Jane Doe", no doubt? In any case, I now find myself in a bit of a dilemma: how do I get out of this hospital without anybody noticing, and without anybody stopping me? It's not as if I can just call somebody? I have no money... I have no car... I have no clothes... I have no phone – so, how the hell am I going to get out of here? From my view of the outside world, through the nearby window, I can see that I must be on the third floor of the hospital? So there is no chance of simply climbing out of the window and making a run for it? So, what am I going to do? What am I going to do? I thought.

Then, before I had a chance to think of another route of escape, a young female nurse came into my room pulling an electronic monitor behind her.

"Hello there! How are you feeling? It's good to see you up and moving around! Are you hungry? Thirsty, maybe? Can I get you anything in particular?" Asked the smiling brown-haired nurse, whose nametag read: "Nurse Jones"?

Sure! I thought to myself. *Sure, why don't you just tell me the fastest way to get out of here, maybe?*

"I just need to take some vitals. I just need to check your heart-rate and your blood-pressure, ok?" Said Nurse Jones, as she proceeded to put a Velcro-fastening cuff around my left-arm that had a cable attached to it that was connected to the blue monitor that the nurse had brought into the room with her.

"No! Wait!" I shouted – before Nurse Jones could turn on the monitor.

"Are you ok? What's the matter?" Asked Nurse Jones with concern in her voice, as the fingers of her left-hand hovered over the buttons of the monitor's control panel.

"Listen, Nurse Jones, I'm going to be honest with you here: I am really not supposed to be here. I don't remember how I got here, nor when – but I still remember who I was... what I was before everything went black, and then I woke up in this bed. So, I need you to do something for me: get me out of here?"

"I can tell that you have been through a very traumatic time? When you were found I am told that you weren't wearing any clothes, and you were sprawled out in the middle of a busy road? You are very lucky to not have been hit by a car or something? I don't know from who, or from what, you were running from – and I do not mean to pry; but, if I were to guess, I would say that you must have been assaulted by someone? Am I right? By your boyfriend? By your husband, perhaps? When you were brought in we naturally called the police, as is customary when someone is found in a similar state as the one in which you were found – and, when you are ready, the police would like to ask you some questions, if that is alright? But only when you are ready?" Said Nurse Jones with a smile.

Nurse Jones was just doing her job, no doubt – but the police? The police were there? And they wanted to talk to me? They must think that I have been sexually-assaulted, or something? Which, I suppose, would be a natural assumption to explain why I was lying naked in the middle of the road when I was found by whomever it was who found me?

"Nurse Jones?" I said, as I looked into her green eyes.

"Natalie," Nurse Jones replied with a smile.

"Natalie? Natalie, please – I need you to get me out of here?"

"Why?" Asked Nurse Jones with a look of concern on her face. "Are you in trouble?"

"You could say that?" I replied.

"How?" Asked a genuinely compassionate Nurse Jones.

"I can't tell you – but I can't stay here any longer. I need to leave this hospital and get home a.s.a.p.!" I replied, as I swung my legs around to the left-hand-side of the hospital bed, and I began removing the cuff that was still wrapped around my arm.

"But you can't just leave? You need more time to fully recover from whatever happened to you? You need to rest?" Said Nurse Jones, as she attempted to restrain me and simultaneously retrieve the cuff that had fallen to the floor.

"Natalie, I can't! I don't have time! I need to get out of here!" I said, as I jumped out of the bed and then shakily attempted to stand upright on the cold hospital room floor without collapsing – however, I quickly lost my balance and fell backwards onto the bed again.

"You see, I told you – you don't need to leave! You don't need to be going anywhere just yet – not until you are ready and fully-recovered?" Said Nurse Jones, as she put both of her hands upon my shoulders.

"Natalie… Natalie, I know that you are just thinking about my well-being – but I need to leave! I can't continue to waste any more time here than I already have!" I pleaded, as I attempted to stand up from my hospital bed again.

"Why don't you tell me your name? Maybe if you tell me who you are, then we can work out who you are and what you have been through?" Asked Nurse Jones, as she looked me straight in the eye.

"I… I…" I replied hesitantly – almost telling Nurse Jones who I was, but then I stopped myself before I disclosed my name. Even then, I knew that in the situation that I found myself in anonymity was key – especially if I had to do something that I didn't want to do in order to get out of that hospital room and away from the hospital where I found myself… something that I was already quietly contemplating at that point.

"The other nurses and doctors are calling you "Jane Doe" – but that can't really be your name?" Said Nurse Jones – sounding as if she were both asking me and telling me that that was the case.

"My name is not important – but what I have to do is!" I said sternly and with urgency in my voice.

"Look *Jane* – or whatever your real name is – why don't you just stay here and I'll be right back in a couple of minutes with a doctor, and then we can find out what is going on? Ok?" Said Natalie with a wide-eyed smile – which made what I knew I had to do next even harder to do than I already knew it was going to be.

I knew that there was only one way that I was going to be able to leave the hospital without having to answer any awkward questions – which was what precipitated my decision to get up out of bed, and then throw my right-arm around Nurse Jones' neck from behind in an attempt to restrict the airway of her throat just long enough that she would lose consciousness when there was no longer enough oxygen being delivered to her brain.

I hated every moment that I squeezed against Nurse Jones' throat with all my strength. I hated that this was the only option that I could come up with in that moment to get me out of that room and away from that hospital.

As soon as I put all of my weight against Natalie's back she quickly started to fall forwards and on to the hard floor beneath our feet. Natalie continued to struggle to breathe and to break free of my embrace – however, I could feel that she was slowly beginning to lose both her strength and her consciousness… and within moments she was lying motionless on the floor, unconscious, with me lying on top of her.

I knew that I had to both think fast and act fast, before it was discovered what I had done – so I took no more time to ponder my options: I got up as fast as I could, I began to quickly undress from my hospital gown, and then I started to undress Natalie of her Nurse's uniform.

When I was finally dressed and wearing Natalie's uniform, and after I quickly put on her shoes – which were luckily the same size that I normally wear – I just bolted out of the hospital room as fast as I could, and I made my way down the nearest corridor, towards the nearest lift that I could find. And it was as I ran down the corridor that I suddenly realized that I was potentially drawing even more untoward attention upon myself – so I decided to slow down my pace slightly to a brisk walk.

Nobody stopped me in my tracks. Nobody even batted an eyelid in my direction. It was as if the Nurse's uniform that I was wearing was somehow camouflaging my true identity from any kind of suspicion. I felt like I was home-free – until an alarm started to wail all around me, and everybody around me immediately appeared to be in a state of panic. I knew why that alarm was going off – they must have found Natalie in my hospital room. Which was why I did not hesitate to run as fast as I could until I finally reached a set of lift-doors, and I did not hesitate to immediately press the Down button on control-panel next to the doors and call for a lift – and as soon as the lift-doors opened I instantly entered the lift and pressed the button for the Ground Floor on the control panel inside. And when the lift finally reached Ground Level, and the lift-doors opened wide again, I did not hesitate to run out of the lift, out of the hospital, and then across the hospital carpark... and I just kept running and running and running, and I did not plan to stop until I reached home.

However, that was until I was stopped in my tracks by the sudden appearance of a black car with tinted windows in my path – which I almost ran head-first into, had I not seen it when I did at the last second before I made contact with its drivers-side door.
I couldn't see anything through the car's darkened windows – however, I was close enough to see my own face being reflected in the dark glass and the extreme state of alarm in my eyes.

I knew that I had to get away from there. I knew that I had to run away from the hospital before somebody came after me, and before somebody got a hold of me for what I had done – and there was no doubt in my mind that the police must already be on their way. So... so I knew I had to... I had to... I had to run.

However, then the tinted window of the drivers-side door of the black car began to lower itself – and when I looked into the car and I saw the face of the driver, I immediately realized that it was... it was *Him*.

It's Him? The guy? The guy from... The guy from the bookstore? The guy from the book-signing? The guy that I... The tall, long-dark-haired, guy that I... That I...?

"Going somewhere?" He asked, in his entrancing and hypnotic tone of voice.

I could not believe that it was... that it was... that it was Him!

"Can I offer you a lift, perhaps?" He asked, as his dark eyes glistened with speckles of light.

He looked even more handsome and dreamy than he did the first time that I saw him – but maybe that was just a result of my over-active heart-rate at that moment, and the flood of endorphins and adrenaline that I was currently feeling? However, I think the true reason was all him – or a combination of all of the above.

I didn't know what to say. I was lost for words. I was lost for thought. I was – yet again – under the spell of this mysterious man – so much so that it took me a few seconds to say:

"Yes! I... that... that... that would be great!" I replied – before I quickly walked to the other side of the car, I opened the passenger-side door of the mysterious man's Mercedes and I stepped inside without further hesitation.

"Fancy bumping into you here?" My mysterious man... I mean *the* mysterious man said with a smile, as he turned to look at me – while simultaneously starting to drive away from where he had picked me up from. "And while wearing such a fetching uniform? I had no idea that you were moonlighting as a nurse?" Said the mysterious man in black with a smile, as he returned my gaze and then looked me up and down from head to toe.

"I... I... I could say the same? I could say the same for you? Were you... were you at the hospital visiting someone?" I asked, as I nervously turned my attention away from the man in black for an instant to look through the rear-window of the mysterious man's car – however, when I did, I discovered that the rear-window was just as darkened as the side windows of this very expensive-looking Mercedes that I was currently sitting in the passenger seat of.

"I… I was indeed visiting someone, as a matter of fact. But, I have to confess that I did not in my wildest dreams ever think, nor expect, to see you there? Which I account as being a true stroke of divine intervention!" Said the man in black with a grin – the same dreamy and handsome man who I had met in that bookstore not that long ago.

"So, I have to ask: what is it with the nurse's uniform? Nurse? Nurse Jones? Are you really a nurse?" He asked.

My attention was instantly drawn back to the man in black and to his mesmerizing eyes.

"I… I'm… I… look, I am… I… I don't know how to say this, but… but…" I sputtered nervously – feeling as if I had been caught red-handed and might potentially be on the verge of being delivered to the nearest police station.

I kept thinking to myself: *if this man were to find out who he currently had as his passenger – who I was and what I had done – then there was no way of telling what he would say, nor what he would do?*

However, for some reason, when I looked into his eyes, and when I analyzed every inch of his perfect face, I could not help myself from trusting him implicitly. I felt like I could tell him anything. ANY-THING. EVERY-THING.

"It's ok! It is perfectly ok – you don't need to say anything! And you don't need to tell me everything! However, perhaps you could tell me where you want to go? And, let me tell you that I am willing to take you anywhere that you might want to go?" Said the man in black, as he smiled from ear to ear.

"I… I…" I tried to reply – however, I could not think of anything to say, nor anywhere else where I wanted to be. After all, my car was now a broken down heap of junk, as far as I was concerned… Melissa had seemingly run away… and I… I… I was currently a messy maelstrom of emotions who felt like she was finally losing her grip on reality.

I was also honestly considering whether the best course action, and the most fulfilling thing I could do, would be to choose to become the Wolf full-time and leave all my human woes behind. I just needed… I just needed…

"You just need some time. You just need to get some rest, perhaps?" Said the man in black, as he gave a genuine smile of understanding – and as he… as he reached out his left-hand to gently stroke my right-hand that was lying flat on my right-thigh. From the moment that I felt his touch, I felt… I felt… breathless.

"I apologize if this seems too forward of me to say for your comfort-level, but I would like to… I would like to invite you to spend some time with me at my home?" He said in a calming tone of voice – which made me feel instantly as if I did not have a care in the world. However, while I was feeling free of any worries – as well as feeling more than a little aroused – the Wolf had other ideas and seemed to be in a state of agitation within me, as if they wanted me to become them; but there was something stopping them from taking over?

I consciously considered the man in black's very generous invitation – until I listened to the Wolf's concerns, and then I wondered whether the man in black's intentions were nefarious? *Because for all I knew he could be some kind of rapist or something? After all, I didn't know a thing about this guy – I didn't even know his name – and now he turns up as if out of nowhere, and he is now propositioning me into going back to his place so that he can… so that we can… what?*

Something definitely didn't feel right – but… but, oh my god, this man was so handsome! So gorgeous! So… so – and I couldn't stop myself from feeling like I just wanted him to take a hold of me, and… and…

"I… I… look, I really appreciate your gracious offer – but… but… I have no idea who… I… I don't even know who you are? You… you could be anyone, for all I know? How can I trust somebody who I do not even know the name of?" I asked, as I could feel tears start to form in the wells of my eyes.

"Then, let me tell you… let me show you who I am and how I can help you, Olivia?" Said the man in black with a smile, as he turned his head and looked me straight in the eye.

Olivia? He called me Olivia? He… he already knew who I was? He already knew my name? But… but how? And who… who… who was he? And in the mix of other questions, another possibility occurred to me: *What was he?*

"How? How do you know my name?" I asked tentatively.

"Olivia, I… I have been around for a long time, and I have met many people in my life. I have met many creatures of darkness and angels of light – however, it was not until I met you that I instantly realized and recognized that I was looking into the eyes of someone who has been walking the fine line between these sometimes vastly-different worlds, but also someone who has not succumbed fully, nor has pledge allegiance to either side exclusively? I instantly recognized from the moment that I saw you that you are somebody who is constantly carrying around a heavy burden of responsibility? You are someone with many secrets? I too know many secrets – some which are as old as time, but still have yet to be learned and understood. By this I mean to say, Olivia, that I can help you. I can help to relieve you of your burdens?" Said the man in black with glint in his eye.

"You don't know anything about me! Besides my name, you don't know who I am? What I am? What I have done? What I can do? And I… I… I don't know anything about you either? You could be the devil himself, for all I know?" I said, as a feeling of unsettlement within me – fueled by the Wolf's constantly growing need to break out of me – intensified and kept telling me that I needed to get out of that car as soon as I could.

However, despite all that I was feeling – and all that the Wolf was communicating – I… I… I could also feel something else when I looked at the man in black, and something that over-ridded my judgement: something I can only describe as a love, a want, a need, an attraction – on a physical, emotional, and on an almost spiritual-level.

There was a part of me that wanted whatever this mysterious man was selling and had to offer – no matter what it cost me. And yet, at this point, I still did not have any idea who he was, nor what he was.

"My name, Olivia, is Vega – and if I remember correctly you are already one of my biggest fans, are you not?" Said the man in black with an enthusiastic smile.

WHAT? WHAT? I thought to myself, as my mind felt like it was on the verge of exploding.

VEGA? VEGA? As in my favourite author Vega who I have been in love with in a literary sense since I read the first volume of their Vampire Spirit series of books? And the same author who arranged a book-signing, but who didn't show up?

But this… this… this man… this… him. He… He is… He was… This is… I was riding in the passenger seat of the one and only Vega? And he was… Vega… he was… he was who I… who I am… I am… I am in… in…

"I am certain that this realization of my identity may come as somewhat of a shock to you – however, I must tell you that I have been wanting to tell you who I am since the moment I saw you looking at my books in that bookstore?" Said the man in black with a beaming smile.

"I… I… I can't believe this! I can't believe that you are… that you are… that you're *Vega*! *The Vega!?*"

"I am indeed!" confirmed Vega with a grin. "And you… you are Olivia… Olivia Hunter, if I am not mistaken?"

"But, how? What? How do you know who I am?"

"It is a talent of mine – and one that has served me well over the years. I have a knack for knowing who a person is upon our first meeting – and when I met you, I knew exactly who and what you were from the instant that I laid my eyes upon you!" Said Vega – just continuing to smile ecstatically, while also still able to drive as if he was capable of doing so with his eyes closed. And, you know what, no matter what set of traffic lights we encountered along the way each and every one was green – as if our route had been cleared for us.

"I can't believe that you are… that you are *Him?* All this time, it has been you? *Vega? Vega?* Oh my god, I can't believe that you are who you say you are?" I said, as if in a daze of bewilderment.

However, then I considered aloud another possibility:

"Wait a minute? You know that Vega is my favourite author, because you saw me looking at their books when we first met? But, how do I know that you are really him? I'm not being funny, but the fact that you just turned up out of the blue, and now turn out to be my favourite author, after all this time, seems very… seems very coincidental, wouldn't you say? For all I know you still could be anybody? How can I trust you? Why should I trust you?" I asked, as a lightning strike of doubt struck within my heart and made me question, naturally, the validity of the man in black's claim that he was in fact Vega.

"Then let me prove it to you? Allow me to take you somewhere, where there are many touchstones that can validate my identity? As a matter of fact, we are almost at the place which I speak of – may I take you there?" Asked Vega calmly, as he kept both hands on the steering wheel and both eyes fixed unwaveringly upon the road in front of him.

"I… I… where? Where? Where could you take me?" I asked nervously – however, as I could feel myself succumbing to him.

"Home, Olivia! Where my heart lies – and where the truths of my identity are constantly on full-display, but usually for my eyes only!" Replied Vega.

I just sat there: listening, thinking, wishing that I could come up with a logical explanation to what was happening – but, to be honest, I was in no fit state of mind to come up with anything that resembled logic in any way, shape, or form. And though I still did not know categorically that Vega was in fact *Vega*, at this point, I… I… I was so tired of bottling up my emotions and resisting my own needs – and, to be honest, I felt like I had nothing left to lose – which was why I said:

"I… I… ok! Ok, *Vega*! I… I am all yours!" I replied, as a single tear fell from my right eye – as I allowed myself to be taken away on both a physical and metaphysical journey with Vega – while at the same time hoping that Melissa was alright, wherever she was, and that I would see her again.

And, for some reason, I felt like something, or someone, was telling me that I was currently with somebody who might have all the answers to all the questions that I have been afraid to ask since I fell off that precipice that led to me becoming the Wolf and the Wolf becoming me all those years ago.

Chapter Eleven:
"I had no idea"

We arrived at Vega's home just after dark. The outside lights of a large house at the end of a long driveway – that reminded me of how Wayne Manor looked in the original Tim Burton *Batman* film, which I watched over and over again when I was a kid – slowly grew brighter and brighter as we approached them. It seemed, at the time, as if Vega had been deliberately taking his time at arriving at his home – however, it is highly possible that this impression that I had was just all in my imagination.

I was incredibly nervous. I was… I was literally shaking in my seat, as Vega parked the Mercedes directly in front of the double front-doors of his epic and impressive-looking home.

I had no idea that writers were this rich? I mean Stephen King and J.K. Rowling maybe, with all the books that they have written? But, if Vega's house was anything to go by, at least from the outside, then he was not just any writer? He must be a member of the British aristocracy, or something? Maybe even royalty? I thought.

The Mercedes came to a stop. And then Vega quickly opened the drivers-side door, he stepped out onto the gravel-covered driveway, he closed the door behind him – and then, as if by magic, he almost instantaneously appeared on the passenger-side of the car and began to slowly open the passenger-side door to my left. Slowly, Vega revealed himself to me – as I just sat there in the passenger-seat of his Mercedes quivering in a state of unbridled unsettlement.

I looked up at him, and into his eyes – as he stood tall in the darkness with only the slight reflection from the lights outside his home and that of the ambient moonlight upon his eyes to hint that he was really there and not a hallucination. I was… I was completely hypnotized and under his spell by this point – and when he held out his right-hand to me, I did not hesitate to take it and allow myself to be guided out of the car and into the night.

Within no time at all Vega and I were walking through the automatically opening front-doors of his house and entering his home without pause.

Vega's home was decorated in red hues from floor to ceiling – from the décor of his furniture to the colour of his curtains. It was like walking into the crimson realm of someone's, or something's, beating heart – if you want to get all poetic about it.

I lost sight of Vega for a moment, as I looked up and then around at the grand hallway that you walked into when you entered the house directly through the front-doors – which appeared to stretch for miles in front of me. The artwork and sculptures that adorned the walls and were on display, the pattern of the long carpet beneath my feet, were all entrancing to my senses – and that was why I was periodically distracted from keeping track of where I was and where Vega was also.

After walking slowly in silence for a few moments, while bathed in the red lighting that emanated from every direction, I finally heard what I can only describe as a *"wisp"* of sound at the same time that the hairs on the back of my neck stood up – as if I could sense that somebody was standing right behind me.

I slowly turned my head – and then I jumped slightly when I realized that it was Vega who was standing behind me with a smile on his face, with both hands behind his back, and with a look in his mesmerizing – now crimson-colored – eyes which instantly made me shiver… with utter excitement, I might add.

"What do you think?" Asked Vega, as he looked me straight in the eye.

I looked around, and then I returned Vega's gaze – however, all the while wanting to say: *Yeah, it's nice! Very nice!* But, in reality, I couldn't say a word.

"Welcome to my home! Welcome to my sanctuary! Welcome to my palace of peace and solitude! Welcome to the place where I rest… the place where I dream… the place where I write… the place that very few people have visited, or have ever seen!" Said

Vega with an exuberant smile – as I just continued to stare dumbfounded into his sparkling eyes.

"This house has been here for a very long time – and before it another structure once stood right here for a considerable period of time... before it was remade, you could say? And I... well, I have lived here a very long time – even longer than both of the structures that I speak of combined! So, I guess you could say that I know this place as well as I know myself?" Said Vega, as he put his right-hand onto my left-forearm and he began to guide me further down the long red hallway.

"Would you care for something to drink? Something to eat, perhaps? Normally I would have someone prepare you something – however, if you so wish I can easily make a meal for you that I am sure will captivate and satisfy your appetite?"

"I... I..." I tried to talk – but I could not for the life of me make a successful string of cogent and understandable sentences with my mouth; however, on the inside I was screaming (make that the Wolf was howling): *WHERE AM I?* And, *WHY AM I HERE?*

Even though I believed that I had given my full consent to have been brought to Vega's home – I still did not know if I was in a place of safety, or one of peril? After all, I still did not know who Vega was at this point... nor for sure if this man really was Vega?

"Olivia, I... I... I am sure that you are wondering: why I have brought you here? And, I know that you are asking yourself: who am I? And, before anything else happens, I feel bound to tell you a few things about myself: namely, my passions and the world in which I have been at the centre of for most of my existence. However, before that, Olivia, I feel I must tell you something else, something important," said Vega, as he guided me further down the red hallway until we reached a large wooden staircase that appeared to rise in twists and turns as far as the eye could see and into the darkness that lay above. Climbing every step of that staircase was like stepping into the dark of the night-sky outside.

All the while, Vega did not look away from me for a second – it was as if he knew his home so well that even if he could not see where he was going, he always knew where he was.

"Olivia, I am… I have been… from the moment that I laid my eyes upon you, I knew that there was something special about you. And now that I know even more about you, I am convinced that we have always been destined to meet. You see, Olivia, I am older than I appear. I am older than you could know. I have been walking this planet, and I have been surviving in this world, longer than many of my kind – mostly because from the time of my birth, and my subsequent rebirth, I have had a destiny. I have met countless people in my time on Earth – however, you are… you are special: you are a wolf in sheep's clothing – literally!" Said Vega, as I just continued to allow myself to be guided by the hand up the huge staircase – however, it was as I replayed in my mind that last phrase that he used, about me being *"a wolf in sheep's clothing"* that I came out of my daze for a few moments, and I asked:

"You? You know me? You? You know what I am?"

However, Vega said nothing in reply and just continued to lead me up the many steps of the staircase.

Within moments, Vega and I reached the third floor of his mansion-sized home, and then we slowly entered a huge and cavernous bedroom with what looked like a King-sized, wooden four-poster bed at its centre.

The bright light of the moon streamed in through the tall uncovered window, as Vega and I stepped into the bedroom.

"Olivia, I need to tell you something? I need to tell you that I am… I am…" said Vega calmly and slowly – and then he opened his mouth ever so slightly, for an instant, and I saw what I thought were two very sharp looking fangs, protruding from just behind his upper lip, which were definitely longer than any normal human teeth that I had seen before. However, at this point, I did not have a firm grasp on what was real – even when what I saw was right in front of me.

"Olivia, I am… I am in love with you! I am so… so… so absolutely ensorcelled and intoxicated by you, that I can no longer hide the truth of my feelings for you. I… I… I have not felt this way for a long time. Of course, I have written about this kind of love in my books – but I have not experienced this kind of instant intoxication for many years. You are… you are the object of my affections and the love that I have been waiting for! You are a creature of the night – just as I am!" Said Vega, as he guided me over to the four-poster bed – and then he stopped, and then he stared at me in perfect silence for a few moments, just before he and I sat down on the giant bed and he leaned in close to my face, and then he said:

"Olivia, I... I..." said Vega, as he put both of his hands on either side of my face, he closed his eyes – as I closed mine – and then I felt the gentle touch of his lips against mine... and then we... and then we...

It all happened so fast. It all happened so spontaneously – one moment we were sitting on the edge of the bed, and then the next we were... we were... we were having sex.

It was wild. It was passionate. It felt... it felt dangerous, at times; however, most likely due to my inability to stop myself from being totally dominated by Vega's tangible hunger, and his need to give pleasure – while at the same time seemingly taking pleasure from every moment of our lustful, exciting, breathtaking, sexual maelstrom and dance with one-another.

I too could not help myself from "taking over", at times, and naturally attempting to dominate Vega and take control over every position and opportunity to show pleasure, and to seek pleasure for myself.

We must have made love for the majority of the night, and for most of the hours of the early morning, in almost complete darkness – with only the twilight glow of the moon and the stars for illumination – and every second felt unbelievable! Incredible! Phenomenal! Fantastic! And I never wanted it to end for anything!

The way he touched me, the way that he caressed my skin... the way he felt was mind-blowing and overwhelming to every one of my senses and my instincts! His tenderness... his voracity, when the moment called for it... his instincts – the way that he knew what to do and when – told me that he was somehow able to read my mind and my body-language sufficiently enough for him to be able to act like I was his every and only desire.

It was like we were two flames of a fire within a raging and bubbling volcano of hot lava – because it was hot, it was uncontrollable, it was explosive, and it was like nothing else I had ever known – and, for my part, I can tell you that I was totally and utterly in love with Vega, as we both shared our bodies, our hearts, and our spirits with one-another.

Eventually, Vega and I did just lay there with one-another and in each other's arms – periodically just looking into each other's eyes and kissing each other on the lips, without even uttering a single word... however, somehow knowing what we were both thinking.

I could not help myself – no matter how impulsive it might seem to someone else listening to this story... I... I really and truly had fallen deeply in love with Vega, over and over again – before we had even met, after we had met, and when we first made love all night long and into the early morning.

Vega's greatest gift was that he could easily take my breath away – even if it were only with a single stare. He was breathtaking – and when he touched me, he honestly made every one of the hairs on my skin stand on-end, as if his hands were able conduct electricity.

•

Just as the early morning light began to shine just below the horizon, I awoke to find that Vega was nowhere to be found and I was alone, as I lied comfortably in his giant silk sheeted four-poster bed. I looked up to the tall window that appeared to stretch from floor to ceiling, and as I did – and as I took a deep intake of breath – I looked on, completely hypnotized, by the golden and majestic light of the sun rising... until the curtains seemingly decided to automatically start to close all by themselves and obscure my view and my opportunity to witness the dawn of a brand new day.

When the blood-red curtains did finally close to completely cover the huge window behind them, the whole room was soon bathed in red light as a burst of what must have been sunlight started to shower through the red curtains – and I felt as if I were waking up from a dream, while at the same within another dream.

The explosive light from the new day's sunrise diminished in intensity almost immediately – and for more than a few moments I just lay there where I was in a state of complete and utter contentment. I felt as if I knew I shouldn't be where I was, but I was glad that I was where I was – if that makes sense? And I didn't even think to worry about anything, because I was so in my element... and because I had never felt so enlivened.

The Wolf? The Wolf was still there, of course – but they were now again in the shadows of my soul, as if they were sulking at the fact that I had made what to them was an act of selfishness? And though I was sorry that the Wolf was seemingly disappointed in my actions, I still did not regret anything that had happened. Making love to Vega, and Vega making love to me, made me feel happier than I had felt in a long time.

I laid in silence for what seemed like a full hour, and then I heard the *click* and the *clack* of a door latch – and soon after I felt the caress of Vega's lips upon my neck, as he approached me from behind, and I... I just closed my eyes, I breathed in deep, and I felt another overwhelming flood of emotions and feelings of excitement, which peaked when he put his mouth up to my left-ear and he whispered:

"Good morning, Olivia!"... And I... I was unable to control myself from smiling from ear to ear, as my heart was beating rapidly in my chest. And then I felt this uncontrollable want and need to see Vega's face again, and to kiss him on the lips – which is exactly what I did, immediately after I rolled over and I met his mesmerizing gaze, and I stroked his face on either side with the thumbs of both of my hands. And then, after I finally forced myself to pull away from his lips and his amazing kiss, I just laid there looking up at him – as I analyzed ever millimeter of his perfect and handsome face. He was... he was unlike anybody I had ever known, or had ever met. He was like a god to me in that moment, as I looked into his eyes and as deep into his soul as I could.

"Hello!" I replied, as I stared into his eyes.

"How are you?" Asked Vega with a smile, as he stared into my eyes and he gently stroked the right-hand-side of my face.

"I'm... I'm great!" I replied with a smile, as I tried to control the raging storm of emotions within me from breaking free and manifesting themselves into a hysterical-sounding giggle of complete and utter happiness and elation.

"Did you sleep?" Asked Vega, as he sat down on the bed beside me.

"I... well, to be honest, not really!" I replied, as I continued to grin from car to car. "Maybe an hour, if I were to guess?" I said, as I propped myself up on to the bed with my left-arm and I sat up to meet Vega's gaze. "You? Did you sleep?"

"I... I did, in a manner of speaking – however, sometimes this soft bed is far too comfortable for me to sleep in. And how could I, or anybody, possibly sleep when they have a beautiful woman like you in their bed?" Replied Vega with a handsome smile.

He was so handsome, so charming... he was such a... such a... such a "lady-killer" – if you know what I mean? He always knew all the right things to say to make my heart race away with itself.

"Really?" I replied; "Is that right?" I asked playfully, as I smiled gleefully. "I bet... I bet you say that to all the women who find themselves in this bed?" I said jokingly – however, after I said it I saw a noticeable change in Vega's facial expressions, as if what I had said had affected him emotionally to the degree that his almost constant warm smile quickly faded into a disparaging grimace.

Vega got up off of the bed, he stood up, and then he looked down upon me.

"Why? Why would you say such a thing?" Vega replied – noticeably annoyed.

"Excuse me?" I said. "What? What did I say?" I asked with surprise in my voice – because, at the time, I was truly oblivious to what I might have said to offend Vega.

"Do you? Do you think that I invite everybody and anybody to share my bed with me? Do you? Do you think that I would choose to have sex with anybody who caught my eye? Do you? Do you think that I... that I open my heart and my home to just anyone?" Said Vega angrily – and he was very angry... and rightfully so, I have to say.

67

"As I told you last night, very few people have been given the privilege of being invited into my home. I told you last night that you… that you are special, Olivia! So, why? Why? Why would you question my intentions?" Said Vega, as he stood with his hands upon both of his hips – and so angry, quite understandably, because at the time he was under the false belief that I thought I was merely the latest in a long line of other women who Vega had invited back to his home to sleep with.

"I… I… I was only joking! I… I… I'm sorry! I'm sorry!" I said – desperately trying to convince Vega and alleviate him of any fear that he may have that I believed he only had nefarious reasons for inviting me into his home and his bed.

"I'm sorry!" I said again, as I kneeled on the bed and I attempted to reach up my right-hand so that I could lay it upon the left-hand-side of Vega's face. "Please… please, forgive me?"

"Olivia, I… I do not want you to ever think of me in such a way. I… I am… there are many things about me that you do not know – and I am by no means an angel… far from it, in fact! I am the antithesis of heavenly – however, I… I… what I want you to know is that to me you are not just anybody! To me, you are special – for many reasons! But… but I can understand why… why you might not believe me – after all, you… you do not really know me, do you? You don't know who, nor what, I am?" Said Vega, as he allowed my right-hand to touch his face ever so slightly so that I could feel the softness of his skin.

"I'm sorry! I… I… I have never met anybody like you in my life! It has been… it has been a very long time since anybody made me feel as amazing as you do! Believe me, I do not think you just pick up women willy-nilly off of the street every day! It's just that all this… you… it all just seems so magical and amazing, and I find it hard to believe that it is all really happening! And… and if you truly knew who I was, and what I was… what I had been through, and what I am still going through every day – then maybe you would understand why… why I would be so… so…" I replied with regret in my voice, as tears started to fall from my eyes.

"It's… it's alright, Olivia! I… I do understand that at this moment in your life everything might seem as if your whole world has been turned upside-down? After all, I know more than you think I do. And that is why... that is why I think... why I think it is time that you returned home?" Said Vega, as he took a step back and withdrew his face from my touch – as I felt like the bed and the entire floor beneath me had just fallen away.

"I... I will make arrangements for you to be returned to your home. And I... I will arrange for someone to retrieve your car from the school where you work and have the much needed repairs made to it to allow it to be driven effectively. I... I... I too am sorry, Olivia!" Said Vega – solemnly and with both hands behind his back – as he took a further step away, until he was out of my reach.

I just sat there in silence: replaying, taking in, and trying to make sense of what Vega had just said – his... his unmistakable rejection of me, and seemingly all because of that stupid joke that I made? That stupid conclusion that I drew?

And then... and then, I watched Vega turn his back on me, and walk away from me and out of the bedroom – leaving me behind and alone, as I attempted to come to terms with the reality of what had just happened.

Soon after, someone – a young man dressed in a black suit, a white-shirt, and a black-tie – who I guessed at the time was someone who worked for Vega – came walking into the bedroom carrying some clothes with both hands. They didn't say anything to me initially, as they made eye-contact with me – as I continued to sit on the bed in silence with a million-and-one things racing through my mind. The Wolf, however, did not make any kind of sound whatsoever from the shadows – which made me feel even more alone and rejected.

The young man in the suit – who looked late-twenties, if I were to have guessed his age from that first appearance – said nothing for a few more seconds, and then he said calmly:

"We have a car waiting for you outside. Preparations have been made for your vehicle to be towed to a garage, where it will be fixed – and when the necessary repairs have been made it will be returned to you. We have arranged for some clothes to be procured for you, so that you may wear something when you leave – and we will shortly dispose of the uniform that you were previously wearing when you arrived here, unless you too would like it returned to you?" Said the snooty-sounding young man – who sounded like he had had a silver spoon quite firmly placed into the side of his mouth for the majority of his life.

And then, as quickly as he entered the room, the young blond-haired man turned around and left.

As I watched the young man walk away, I was… I was angry – to say the least. I was annoyed. I was in a state of disbelief. And I was more than a little depressed also – to tell you the truth. I didn't know what to think, I didn't know what to do – but I decided to take the hint that I was being given, and I got up out of bed and I started to get dressed into the clothes that had been given to me: a knee-length red satin-dress, and some black, slightly-heeled, shoes – which actually fit me surprisingly well.

And then I waited on the bed, until the young man returned and then waved with his right-hand for me to follow him – and then, slowly but surely, I was escorted down the staircase that I had climbed the night before, down the red-decorated hallway all the way to the giant double-doors that were the front-door of Vega's house, and then I… I left.

When I walked out into the bright sunlight there was a black Mercedes waiting for me – similar to the one that Vega had been driving when he picked me up from outside the hospital yesterday – and I did not hesitate, nor question that it was for me, as I pulled open the passenger-side door and I stepped inside.

I got into the passenger-side of the black Mercedes without uttering a single word, nor without even looking to my right to see who was driving – because I just wanted… I just wanted to get away from that place. However, in retrospect, I was, in all honesty, in two-minds about whether I wanted to leave without… without at least seeing Vega first.

I did not get much time to question if I did in fact want to leave – because more or less as soon as I sat in the passenger-seat of the black Mercedes its driver immediately started to drive away from Vega's house, and the driver did not stop driving for anything until I was back at home.

When I finally arrived home, I opened the front-door of our house with the spare key. I entered. I went upstairs to my bedroom. I stripped myself of the clothes that I had been given to wear. I took off my underwear. And then I laid down on the bed, and I cried myself to sleep.

Chapter Twelve:
"Don't wake me up"

For the next month, I felt like nothing more than a zombie. I went where I had to go, I did what I had to do – but I wasn't really living, or at least I did not feel alive.

For the first few days after I returned home I didn't even leave my bed. I called in to work and I told them that I was suffering from the worst case of the flu I had ever had – but that *"I would make every effort to get well as soon as I could and return to work as soon as possible"*. I called in on the Thursday of that week, and I returned to work the following Monday – arriving on time in my newly fixed and now road-worthy car, which drove as great as the first day I got it.

On my first day back at school, I taught my class, I attended a return to work meeting with the Head Teacher... and then, when school was over, I went home, I ate, I went to bed, I slept... and then, the next morning, I got up, I went to work, I taught my class, and when school was over I went home, I ate, I went to bed... and then the next morning I... you get the idea – I basically just repeated the same cycle over and over again.

On the weekend, I would sleep in till noon – and then I would get up out of bed, sit down at the dining room table, eat something, and prepare the next week's lesson breakdown for my class and organize my work schedule, read through and grade any and all of the home work that my class had completed and submitted – and once I had done what I had to do in order to make it appear that I was the *numero uno* of teachers and that I had everything completely and utterly under control, I laid in bed... I listened to some music on my iPod... and then I cried, and I cried, and I cried.

And then, when the weekend came to an end and the new working week began, I jumped out of bed... I got dressed... I ate some breakfast alone at the dining room table... I drank some coffee... I left the house... I went to work, and I taught my class to the best of my ability.

And that same cycle continued – over and over again, day after day, and week after week – until... until I just... until I just couldn't do it anymore, any of it. I didn't want to go on with my life as it was anymore. And that was when I decided to ask the Wolf for something... that was when I decided to give the Wolf something... something important: me... my life... full-control over our shared fate and destiny.

So, one night, I started talking directly to the Wolf, as I was looking out the window at the full moon in the dark starlit sky – both out loud and internally, and I began by saying:

"I'm sorry! I'm sorry! I guess... I guess I should have listened to you from the start? That's my problem though – I don't ever truly listen? I know that you can hear me. I know that you know I am talking to you – my other half, my spirit, my gift – and you know why? It's not always been easy between us – but over the years we have both come to appreciate each other, so much so that we could not imagine life without one another? You know me, and I know you. And I know that you will believe me when I say that I am done! And that I am... I am willing... I am willing to let go for good and let you take over! I am willing to take a back-seat! I am willing to put Olivia behind me again, and everything about her – her life, her memories, and her emotions – and become the Wolf in every way... to become you, and never choose to return to my human form! I... I just can't live like this anymore! I... I... I want to be free of all this pain that I am feeling! I want to be you! I want you to be me!" I said impassionedly – however, the Wolf said nothing, the Wolf did nothing. Until... Until I closed my eyes, and I said within my mind:

"Your time has come!" – and that was when I felt the Wolf come forward in my mind, for the first time in a long time, and almost breakthrough the threshold of transformation that lay between our two distinct forms; however, just as I prepared myself to change into the Wolf, it was then that I heard an unmistakable voice inside my head as clear as day, which said:

"Help me!" – and that was when the fog of depression lifted slightly, because the voice that I heard was that of my daughter, Melissa... and I quickly concluded that she must be attempting to

communicate with me somehow, one month after she disappeared before my eyes.

"Melissa?" I said out-loud – however, still continuing to stand by the window with my eyes closed. "Where are you?"

I heard nothing for perhaps five minutes – and then, just as I was about to open my eyes, I saw her face… I saw Melissa's face staring back at me, and I heard her say:

"Mum, they've got me!"

"Who's got you?" I asked.

"They're coming! They're coming for you, Mum! They know who you are! They know where you are!"

"Who? Who?" I asked with urgency in my voice.

"I should have told you, Mum! I should have told you what I knew, what I was told! But, I was afraid! I'm sorry! I'm sorry!" Said Melissa apologetically.

"Missy, it's ok! It's ok! Just… just come home! Just come home!" I said.

"I can't! They're coming for you! You've got to run! You've got to get away before they find you, before… before they kill you!" Said Melissa – sounding as if she were in tears wherever she was.

"Who? Who?" I asked again.

"The blood-suckers! The wraiths of darkness! The demons that hide in plain-sight! The… the… the Vampires! They… they got to me, and now they're coming for you! You've got to run! RUN! RUN! RUN!" Said Melissa – before the image of her face disappeared from my mind, and no matter how many times I called out her name she did not reply.

But, who was she referring to? Who came for her? And who was it that was coming for me? And, where was Melissa now? And why did she run away? And why does she want me to run? Vampires, she said? Vampires? What is she talking about? Who is she talking about?

Then I heard the doorbell ringing, which immediately made me open my eyes and turn around to look out the window to see who was at the front-door – and at that late hour? And that was when I saw Him, for the first time in a month, for the first time since he seemingly rejected me and threw me out of his bed and his home… that was when I saw Vega.

He looked up at me, as I looked down on him – and, as Vega and I stared at one another, the Wolf in me made it abundantly clear that they were ready and waiting to come out at a moment's notice. However, for right then, I decided that the best thing to do was to go down stairs, to open the door, and to at least ask Vega why he was outside my house at this late hour.

So, I made my way down the dark hallway to the steps of the staircase – and then, after I reached the front-door of the house, I took my time in unlatching the lock and slowing opening the front-door to reveal the unmistakably handsome face of Vega and his sparkling eyes staring back at me.

"Olivia?" He said immediately with a smile. "How are you?"

"How am I? How am I? You… you have got some nerve, I'll give you that! How am I? How? How dare you? Who are you to treat me the way that you have?" I said, as I stared into Vega's eyes with a scornful expression on my face – at least that was the expression that I hoped I was conveying, because… because I was angry. However, in the same breath, I was also happy to see Vega again.

"And now you turn up on my doorstep? You know… I know who you are – but, I wonder, who do you think *you* are?" I said – and I was about to go off on a further vitriolic rant about even though Vega seemingly had loads of money, that did not mean that he had the right to use people and then cast them aside when he was finished with them. However, I could see in Vega's eyes that he wasn't just stopping by for no reason – which was why I said nothing for a few seconds and I just waited for him to start talking again.

"Olivia, I apologize for turning up unannounced – however, there are matters of great importance that we must discuss. I invited you into my home, and now I ask you to invite me into yours? Time is of the essence, and what we must discuss is a matter of life and death… change and instinct… spirit and destiny. Please?" Said Vega – noticeably apologetic and submissive in his mannerisms and body-language.

I said nothing for a few seconds longer, as I stared into his eyes – as I experienced intense flashbacks in my mind to the night that Vega and I had spent together, and how much it had meant to me, and what he… what Vega meant to me. I wanted to burst into tears – that was my initial instinct in response to what he had said, but instead I just lowered my head slightly and I opened the front-door even wider so that he could enter freely.

I closed the front-door, and then I followed Vega as he walked down the unlit hallway to the kitchen.

"Can I get you anything?" I asked with my arms crossed out in front of me, as Vega stood near the sink with his back to me – seemingly staring out the kitchen window to the back garden.

"No, Olivia, I'm… I'm fine! However, I do have something for you?" Replied Vega, as he slowly turned to face me again.

"May we take a seat?" Asked Vega, as he looked towards the nearby dining-table.

"Sure!" I replied immediately with an indignant smile on my face, as I stood there with what felt like a fire burning inside me – also known as the Wolf. "Why not?" I said, as I followed Vega over to the dining-table – at which we both sat on opposite sides of, as we stared each other in the eye.

"So? So, what is this? What was so urgent that it couldn't wait until, say, tomorrow? Why now? And I'm not even going to ask how you got here, nor how you knew where I lived? I have had a lot of time over the last month to ask myself some very pertinent questions: Who you really are? How you always seem to be in the right place at the right time to run into me? How you already knew my name? And, of course, why? Why? Why invite me back to your home? Why have sex with me? Why leave me alone, and then let your sniveling underling be the one to escort me off of your property – like I was an unwanted guest?" I asked without even a pause for breath – because I was so angry, so annoyed, and yet I was so fascinated to find out what was going on and who Vega really was.

"I'm a vampire!" Vega admitted calmly, and without any further hesitation. "In fact, you could say that I am *The Vampire*? The original – shall we say? I have walked this world for hundreds of years – and as the planet has changed and remade itself over and over again, so too have I! I am a born survivor! I am the father! I am the blood! I am the source! I am the king of my kind – and to my kind, my words are like that of a god – because I am a god in the eyes of my kind!"

"We – *Vampires* – have been written about for centuries. We have a well-known mythology. We have well-documented lusts, vices, weaknesses, and customs – and yet, only a few have wondered: Where did vampires come from? Well, you might as well as ask: Where did humanity come from? It's like asking: Where did all the trees, the birds, the fish, the elephants, the wolves come from? Where did religion come from, and why? Why did God create the universe in the first place? Where did life begin? And what was its first form? Asking: Where do vampires come from? Is like asking: Where do werewolves come from? And you already know the answer to that question – do you not, Olivia?" Said Vega, as he stared at me with a smile on his face – seemingly waiting for me to reply.

However, I was in no fit state of mind and body at the time to talk – because I was, yet again, shell-shocked by what I had just heard… and the most resonating and reverberating of all that Vega had said was all that I could clearly remember: *"I'm a Vampire!"… "I'm a Vampire!"*

And then, something occurred to me:

He just insinuated that I am… that he knows about… he knows that I am… I am…

"But, Olivia – that does not change how I feel about you, nor how much I have been thinking about you?" Said Vega, as he looked into my eyes and attempted to use whatever gift of telepathy he had at his disposal to peer inside my mind and clear my thoughts of the fog of confusion that engulfed them.

The Wolf was absolutely clamoring to break-free, but I would not allow them – not until I heard some more from Vega about who he was and what he was.

"I? You? You're a… you're a…?" I stuttered in reply.

"A vampire? Yes! Yes I am!" replied Vega without hesitation.

"And, you know that I… that I am a…?"

"A werewolf? Yes, I know!" replied Vega immediately.

"But? But, how? Why?" I asked – before I was confronted in my thought process by something that Melissa had communicated to me not that long ago, when we were talking to each other seemingly telepathically:

"The blood-suckers… the vampires… they're coming for you… RUN! RUN! RUN!" she had said.

And then, as I looked into Vega's eyes, it occurred to me:

Oh my god! Oh my god, Vega – the "King of the Vampires" – is sitting at my dining-table, and he must be… he must be here to… to… to kill me?

I could tell – just by looking at Vega's facial-expressions – that he could recognize that there was something wrong with me, and that I was more than a little agitated.

In my mind, at this point in time, I surmised that this situation could only end one of two ways: one, Vega races over to where I am sitting and he bites my neck, sucks my blood, and then leaves me for dead? Or, I let the Wolf out and they leap over the table and they bite Vega's head off before he can do anything? So, no matter what happened, there was either going be Vega's blood spilt all over the dining-room table, or mine – in other words: messy… murderous.

It was as if Vega and I were in the middle of a stand-off – with no indication as to what, or who, was going to end up the victor.

I knew that Vega was somehow reading my mind and he knew exactly what I was going to say, and what I was going to do, before I did – so, I decided to be more like the Wolf, and I waited… I listened… I watched… and I considered all the possibilities that presented themselves to me.

"I can see in your eyes that you have a thousand questions? And I can feel in your heart that you are feeling a million emotions? And I can sense in your soul that the wild one who you share your existence with is clamoring for the light? However, before anything happens, I ask you to listen to me very carefully?

We may not have known one another, as we are now, for long –
however, I have known about you all my life. I know who you are,
I know what you are… and I have encountered many others with
your changeling-like abilities many times."

"I once encountered a woman like you, many years ago, who
could transform herself into a wolf… who sought me out to ask me
for a favor, of sorts – however, I declined her request… and I told
her that I do not engage in matters of the heart, especially when
they pertain to revenge. I believe her name was…" said Vega –
before I interjected, and I said:

"Don't tell me! Don't tell me! Her name was *Tala*, wasn't it?"
I said with a smile, as I could feel my blood start to boil in my
veins.

"You know her?" Asked Vega, as he raised both eyebrows.

"*Knew*… I *knew* her!" I replied sardonically.

"So, she is… she's dead now, I take it?" Asked Vega with a
look of intrigue on his face.

"Yeah, you could say that? She, um… she met her demise at
the teeth of yours truly, in fact! I was the one… I was the one who
stopped that evil witch in her tracks – once and for all! I was the
one who sent that manipulative woman to her grave! Me!" I said
with an air of smugness.

"Really? You? Wow! Wow! It appears that I may have
underestimated you, Olivia? Someone as sweet and innocent as
you? A killer? No, it can't be?" Said Vega, as he stared at me – as
if he were entranced by every word that I uttered.

"Believe it! If you know anything about me, then the one thing
that you should believe to be true is that I am not to be
underestimated!" I replied with a smile, as I leaned forwards and I
put both of my hands flat on the dining-table. "In all my years as
the Wolf… as a mother… as a survivor… as a predator… as a
protector… as a student… as a teacher – I have learned that I can
change, adapt, and overcome any and every obstacle in my path!"
I said with pride and passion in my unwavering voice.

"I agree! I agree!" Said Vega with grin and with a slight nod
of the head. "And it was your spirit, your heart, your strength, your
soul, that immediately drew me to you – and which brought me to

you tonight. I have come to you, because I love you – and because I believe that you and I are kindred-spirits, and together you and I could become something incredible!" Said Vega.

My heart fluttered extravagantly in my chest – which slightly subdued the anger that I was still feeling at that moment.

He just said that he loved me! He loves me?

And the more that I thought about what Vega had said, the more that I felt as if I were again slowly falling under his spell.

The Wolf, however, was anything but subdued – they wanted out. And I believe that it was the Wolf who kept repeating in my mind:

Melissa... Melissa – and it was as a result of that that I immediately came-to again, and the reason why I just snapped back by saying:

"Really? Really? Well, what about Melissa? Huh? What about my daughter? You see, I would probably take what you have got to say as Gospel – if I had not already been alerted that some *blood-suckers*, some *vampires*, were already on the way, who are coming to get me for God knows what reason!" I said – angry as hell – as I stared into Vega's eyes and I attempted to communicate every ounce of anger and annoyance that I was feeling – while simultaneously struggling to keep the Wolf from breaking-through, which was getting harder and harder to do with every passing minute. I think the Wolf was angrier than I was – and that was saying something.

Vega looked almost shocked by what he had heard – if I were reading his facial expressions accurately.

"Olivia?" Vega began – before I cut him off.

"Don't! Just don't! Don't tell me anymore lies, because I don't want to hear them!" I said, as I stood up from the dining-table and I looked down at Vega. "What I want... what I really want is for you to get up, to get out of my house, and to go back to wherever you came from – and I want you to leave me alone! I am sick of being used by people! I am sick of living with the feeling of having a shadow hanging over me! I am sick of running!"

"So, this is the deal: you leave and never come back – and while you are doing that, you get on the phone and you call whoever is holding my daughter against her will and you tell them to release her! Or, you leave and I find out where Melissa is by myself – and after I do I am going to find you, and every other vampire I can find, and I am going to hunt you all to extinction! I'm telling you right now that if she has been hurt in any way, you will suffer my wrath! You got all that? Or, do you need me to repeat myself?" I said – almost howling afterwards, as if I were merely a megaphone for the Wolf's silent intentions, coupled with that of my own anger over the thought of Melissa being imprisoned seemingly by the vampire currently sitting at my dining-table.

"Olivia? Olivia?" Said Vega, as he attempted to start talking again – however, this time he was interrupted by the sudden sound of people outside the house... which I too heard, as well as sensed.

And then what sounded like a car-alarm started to wail – and that was enough of a trigger to make me start changing into the Wolf. However, just as I was beginning to change, I felt a sudden shock to my system overcome me – and within no time at all I lost consciousness and everything went dark. And as I drifted away, I distinctly heard Vega say: *"I am not your enemy"* – but, at the time, I couldn't tell who he was talking to.

Chapter Thirteen:
"Out of body"

What happened next could only be described as an out of body experience – because when I regained my vision I could actually see myself lying on the floor, seemingly unconscious, and I could also see Vega and a large group of men and women dressed in black and dark-grey attire all standing in my dining-room and having what looked like a very heated discussion. They were saying something to Vega – however I couldn't hear what they were saying, because it was as if my hearing had become muted somehow… it was as if they were moving their mouths but no sound was being produced.

After a few moments, my ability to hear what was being said did eventually return – however, by that time, I seemed to have missed a lot of what had already been said, because the first thing that I heard when my hearing was restored was:

"Do you understand, your majesty?" – And that question was being asked by who I assumed was the leader of the group who had broken into my home.

"Do you actually believe that this insurrection will succeed in anything but signing your own death warrants? Do you think you are the first to challenge my leadership and authority? Do you all actually believe that any of you are going to leave this house alive? How dare you? How dare you? Who do you think you all are?" Said Vega, angrily, as he looked into the eyes of each and every one of the people standing in my kitchen and dining-room.

"My king, you are weak! You are in no position to threaten any one of us. You have no right to question what we have done, nor what we will do next. Our actions are for the betterment of our race. And your *leadership*, as you call it, is an embarrassment to us who believe that you are steering us down a path of extinction," said the same man who spoke before – who I assumed was the ring-leader of this group of what appeared to be rebel vampires who appeared to be staging a little *coup d'état* against Vega.

It was just after the rebels' leader finished speaking that Vega just burst into a fit of laughter – which took everybody in the room by surprise, me included, because it just came out of nowhere. Vega's laughter served effectively at breaking the level of tension in the room – as did his ear to ear smile that he wore as he stood with his hands on his hips.

"My children, you know nothing!" Said Vega, as he made sure to look into the faces of everybody in the room.

"Do you know who I am? Do you know how long I have lived? Do you know what I have done? Where I came from? No? I am your god! I am responsible for your creation! I am the first, and I will be the last! I know each and every one of your faces – and I will not let any of you spread your poisonous rebellion any further!" Said Vega with a look of complete and utter annoyance – though sounding strangely amused as he spoke.

"You are too late, your majesty – we are but the start! We have been following you… we have had spies within your midst for months – those like us who believe that your fire burns now for this pathetic human female rather than for the continuation of your people!" Said the very rude and obnoxious leader of this rebellion, as he stepped forwards and looked directly into Vega's – while simultaneously pointing his right-hand in the direction of my motionless human body lying on the dining-room floor.

"Pathetic human female", eh? I thought, as I began to make a mental list of who I was going to kill first – if I ever returned to my body.

"We have her daughter!" He said.

"Where?" Asked Vega, as his smile faltered and his facial expressions instantly became a look of contempt.

"I'm afraid that information is need to know, your majesty – and soon you will have no need to know anything of the kind!" Said the rebel vampire, who was holding my daughter hostage against he will – who I was beginning to realize that Vega only had a passing association with, besides them both being vampires.

"You see, your majesty – every vampire in this room is no longer your subordinate... we no longer take orders from you, and we never will again!" Said a female vampire, as she stepped forwards to look Vega in the eye.

"Val? I never thought that I would see the day when you would question me, nor seek to overthrow me? I do not know how you were drawn into all this, nor what you were promised – however, I promise you that if you help me stop whatever this is, now, then I will spare your life!" Said Vega to Val – the beautiful female vampire who Vega appeared to be personally familiar with.

"My king, I am not easily turned – as you know. My allegiance is now with those who want a new beginning for our race – beyond what came before... beyond the shadows... beyond you! From the moment that you became obsessed with *her* – this inferior human slut," said the female vampire – who instantly made it on to my mental kill-list with that *"inferior human slut"* remark. "Since the moment you chose to consort with this lesser species..."

"Lesser species?" Replied Vega immediately; "Lesser species? A lesser species who you were all one of, once upon a time?"

"Once – before we ascended to the superior race that we are now! I would think that you of all people would agree with that statement, your majesty?" Said the same male rebel vampire standing in front of Vega along with "Val".

"Superior?" Vega replied, as if flabbergasted by the male vampire's assertion.

"Are we not? Is that not what you and the other elders of our race have been preaching for hundreds of years?" Said the male vampire.

"My child, you are superior to no one! And your actions here tonight are proof-positive of that fact!" Said Vega, as he continued to wear his contemptuous smile.

"No, your majesty – it is your subversive actions that are proof that you are no longer superior! Coming to this human's home... only a month ago inviting them into your home... having sex with this human female – instead of doing what vampires do and have been doing for all of our history: hunting our human prey, killing, and then draining them of every last drop of their blood and taking everything that made them who they were, and transforming their life-force into our own being so that we may continue to thrive!" Said the male vampire, as he flashed his sharp vampire fangs. "That is the true vampire way!"

"Things change!" Said Vega, as he pulled back his chair and then sat down again – as he looked up and met the eyes of each and every one of the vampires in the room.

"Things change – and each of you know that better than anybody, because each and every one of you was once human… and each of you, to this day, still continue to live as if you were human – when you are not acting like rebellious vampires?" Said Vega calmly.

"Take you, Val – who are you? What are you?" Asked Vega, as he focused his attention solely upon Val.

"I am a vampire!" Replied Val, passionately and without hesitation.

"Yes, yes you are – however, most of the time, you are a…? You are lawyer, if I am not mistaken? You are 250 years-old – and for most of your time on Earth you have had an intense fascination and obsession with the rule of law, and an understanding of why rules and laws are necessary to any society? And you know better than I that every country on this planet has their own distinct laws that define who they are as a people – just as vampires do?"

"However, though we are our own race, vampires do not have our own individual country to call our own – because we are from everywhere. England? The United States of America? France? Russia? China? South America? Australia? There is even a scientist, who is a vampire, doing research as we speak on the continent of Antarctica! Vampires in space! Vampires below the ocean! Vampires of all shapes and sizes, colour and ethnicity – who all count themselves as being a Vampire first and foremost, above all else!"

"Being who we are is both a gift and a curse. Living on this planet of light and dark is a constant test for each of us. However, every day and every night we rise to our potential."

"Some vampires can be out in the daylight for hours at a time before their skin starts to show signs of mottling, and begins to burn from their exposure to the ultraviolet radiation – while others spontaneously-combust instantly when exposed to direct sunlight? Skin protection… umbrellas… only going outside during the hours of twilight… hats, gloves, sunglasses – some would say that you are not a true modern vampire unless you do not worry about these things, nor if you do not take precautions against this sometimes inhospitable world – at least if you are a vampire?"

"That has been our story… that has been my story since the moment of my birth and rebirth. Nothing worthwhile ever comes easy – and life is sometimes the hardest thing to live through. Vampires live in the shadows, because we must! Vampires do not expose themselves unless they must! There are humans who know more about us than others – there are leaders of whole countries who are vampires, after all? And, yes, we will all always drink blood… we will always feed when necessary, and some too will always hunt – but we are more than those stereotypical attributes, and that has always been my belief."

"We are not animals! We are not human! We are Vampires! And take it from me, what sets us apart from everything and everyone else is our strength of identity and our sense our purpose. We can do anything!" Said Vega, as he basically told every vampire within the reach of his voice – and me also – the facts of vampire life: all of which I was both surprised by and enlightened by – especially by the realization that Vampires were real, that they were their own race of people, that they had their own history, that they had their own ethos to life, and that they had their own trials and tribulations that they had to face. Vega was incredibly articulate and well-spoken – no wonder he was such a fantastic writer.

"Yes, your majesty – you are so right! So right! We are vampires! We do have a strength of identity and purpose! And, yes, we can do anything! Thank you! Thank you!" Said the male vampire standing directly in front of Vega – before… before… before, within the blink of an eye, he quickly threw himself forwards and plunged what looked like a shard of black-glass into Vega's chest and immediately knocked Vega back in his chair.

I was... I was... I was in shock! I was... I was... I was angry. I was instantly incensed – but no matter what I was feeling, I knew that there was nothing that I could do... because at that moment in time I was... I was the Wolf – in spirit only, you could say? I was out of my body... I was out of my mind... and I could not interact with whom I was seeing, nor could I do anything about what I was seeing. Vega too looked in shock, as he sat there in his chair with a huge shard of black-glass jutting out from his chest.

The male vampire took a step back from Vega, as if he were afraid of what was going to happen next – as did everybody else in the room.

"Vincent? Vincent?" Said "Val" with what sounded like urgency in her voice, as she looked at "Vincent" – who continued to look at Vega unflinchingly.

I too could not take my eyes away from Vega – as he... as he looked as if he... as if he were... dying – as his eyes flickered, and as blood started to drip from the corner of his mouth.

Vega did not say a word... he just sat there, seemingly in pain – and then... and then... and then he looked at me, as I was looking at him – in my spirit-form, and not in my physical form – as if he... as if he were the only one in the room who could see me. I didn't know if he could really see me – but, at that moment, that was what it seemed like... that was what it felt like, because... because he was looking right at me.

However, then... then... then Vega closed his eyes – and it was then that I realized that he... he was dead.

"Vincent? Vincent?" Said Val again, as she started to pull against Vincent's black coat. "We have to go! We have to leave!" Said Val, as she tried to pull Vincent towards the hallway that lead back to the front-door – as the rest of the group began to retreat and leave my house.

"What do we do now? What do we do with them?" Asked Val, as she continued to pull at Vincent's coat.

"I... I..." sputtered Vincent, as the coward tried to reply.

"We have to leave! We have to go!" Val repeated.

"I... I..." sputtered Vincent again – before he regained some semblance of conscious irrationality, and then he replied: "Burn them! Burn them! Burn the bodies! Burn the house! Set... set this place alight! If they want to be together that much, let them die together! Let them know... let there be nothing left of them but ash!" Vincent almost screamed, as his eyes grew wide and wild, and as his nostrils flared – in other words: the psychotic and murderous vampire was going all-in on death and destruction.

"But, we... we can't just leave them like that?" Said Val; "Why don't we feed on them first? Then sacrifice them, as is customary..."

"As is customary? Do you hear yourself? There is no custom... there is no president for any of this! I have killed a king... a god! Nobody in all our history has done such a thing! I am... I am... we must do what has never been done! And from the flames a new king will rise!" Said Vincent – in total psychopath-mode at this point.

Then, Val looked as if she were reaching to bite the left-hand-side of Vega's neck – before Vincent grabbed her, before she could get too close, and then he pulled her away.

"No!" Shouted Vincent, angrily. "No! Burn them! Now!" Said Vincent – and then he and Val raced down the hallway towards the front-door, leaving Vega and me alone in the dining-room.

I knew that if I was going to do something, anything, I was going to have to do it immediately, and fast – because I believed that these rebel vampires wholeheartedly meant everything that they said.

However, for some reason, I still felt paralyzed and unable to return to my human body. I was like a ghost – but I knew that I couldn't live like this forever, and that time was definitely of the essence.

I looked at Vega again, sitting lifeless in his chair, and I mourned silently for him – and then I asked him to help me find a way to save myself, to save Melissa, and to stop the rebel vampires out there before it was too late.

"Vega, wherever you are, I hope you can hear me – because... because I need to tell you something. I... I need to tell you that... that I'm... I'm sorry! I should have believed you! I should have trusted you! But, in all honesty, you can't blame me for not believing you – because, up until now, I don't think I actually knew who you really were? But, even before now, I knew... I knew that I loved you! I guess I fell for you from the moment I started reading your books? And though we only got to know each other for a short time, if at all, I... I just want you to know that... I really do love you! I can't explain... I can't make sense of it – but when I look into your eyes it is as if I have always known you, and I have always loved you... as if we knew each other in another life? Or something like that? I know all that might sound crazy, but it's true! And that is exactly how I feel about you! I never, in my wildest dreams, thought that I would actually get to meet you – let alone fall in love with a real-life vampire! But that is exactly what happened from the moment that I laid my eyes upon you... and, believe me, I will never forget you! But, if you are still out there somewhere, I... I need you... I need you to help me return to my body, so that I can help my daughter, and avenge you also – because whoever these vampires are they need to be stopped! Please, Vega, help me? Please, God, help me to get out of this? Someone, something, please! Please! Please!" I said... I explained... I pleaded, as I looked at Vega – however, in truth I did not expect any kind of response from him.

After a few seconds of just standing there in silence, that was when the first of many Molotov cocktails – I guess you would have to call them – came flying and smashing their flammable and explosive contents into the kitchen. A destructive fire soon erupted and began to spread the more Molotov cocktails were thrown into the house. It truly did feel like that was going to be it for me, for Vega – and God only knew what was going to happen to Melissa?

I was about to start saying my goodbyes to everyone I had ever loved, and attempting to reach out to Melissa telepathically if I could – when I saw something: a face in the flames of the now raging fire.

I saw… the face… I saw the face of Vega – and then, slowly but surely, Vega's entire body materialized and walked out of the flames until he was within touching distance.

I didn't immediately know at the time whether who I was seeing, or what I was seeing, was a ghost or a hallucination – however, when this apparition of Vega began to speak directly to me, I knew that they… I knew that it was Him… I knew they were Vega.

"Hello again, Olivia!" Said Vega with a smile, as he crouched down to look me in the eye. "Yes, I can see you – and, yes, I always knew you were there!" Said Vega, as he kissed me on the nose.

"So, this is the Wolf? May I say that you look magnificent! Amazing! Beautiful! Not only when you are human, but when you are the Wolf as well!" Said Vega, as he stood up, he looked down, and he admired me.

"I would like to tell you more about who I am, and what I am – but, as I said to you a long time ago now, you and I are not that dissimilar from one-another. And now, you and I must return to our bodies before it is too late – so that we may stop what I foresaw was always going to happen!"

"Vega?" I thought, as I stared up at him; *"How? How?"*

"There will be time for explanations later – however, for right now, we must wake up!" Said Vega – immediately before he turned around on the spot and reached out his right-hand to touch the head of his physical body – and then… and then it was as if he "leaped" back into his body, which was still impaled by that large shard of black-glass.

Immediately after he regained consciousness in his physical body again, and after he realized where he was, Vega took a hold of the shard of black-glass in his chest and he pulled hard at it until he was again free of its sharp edges. And after a few moments – during which it appeared as if he were trying to catch his breath – Vega then threw the black-glass away and into the flames of the fire that was quickly beginning to engulf the entire house.

As soon as Vega caught his breath sufficiently, he immediately turned to where I was standing, he smiled, and then he got up out of the chair that he was still sitting on and he went over to where my human body was lying on the floor and he put his right-hand onto my head.

I remember seeing this intense flash of light – and then, within the blink of an eye, I was opening my eyes again in my human body and immediately coughing profusely because of the amount of smoke that I was inhaling… because of the fire raging around us that was getting closer and closer with every passing second.

Vega slowly helped me to my feet. We held each other. We looked into each other's eyes. We kissed one-another on the lips. And then, seemingly without even a second thought, Vega broke the double-glazed dining-room window with one blow from his right-hand – and then, as the smoke alarms blared, Vega and I escaped from the burning house that was once Melissa and my home.

Vega and I raced around the side of the house to the front-driveway – and then, hand-in-hand, we made a run for his black Mercedes that was parked a little further down the road – as the entire neighborhood of people who lived on our street started running out of their houses also to witness the fire that continued to burn and spread through every room faster than anything I had ever seen.

When Vega and I got into the black Mercedes, he seemed no worse for wear – however, on the other hand, I was more than a little out of breath and feeling the damaging side-effects of carbon-monoxide inhalation: my lungs felt like they were on fire, as did my throat. However, after a few seconds of just sitting there and breathing in fresh air, I did begin to feel extremely better in no time at all.

When I turned my head to the right to look in Vega's direction, I immediately saw that he was looking at me also – with a look in his eye that instantly made me smile and my heart race away with itself. And after a few more seconds of just staring at one-another, both Vega and I leaned-in, in perfect synchronicity, and we met each-other's lips – and, let me tell you, that unbelievable and amazing kiss lasted longer than I could ever estimate… because it was phenomenal! It was incredible! And it was just what we both needed after what we had just been through.

Just before sunrise, Vega and I drove away from the street where Melissa and I used to live – dodging all the people still standing on the street, and all the fire-engines that were parked on the road – and then we made our way to Vega's house.

When we arrived at Vega's home – just as the sun began to peak over the horizon – we wasted no time in entering his lavish and impressive house. As soon as we walked through the front-door, we both decided – as if telepathically – to take some time and get some much needed rest to recover from the events of the previous night, but... but not before Vega and I picked up where we left off a month ago, and we... and we showed each other just how much we loved one-another. And, I swear to God, we didn't leave each other's sight for two days straight.

Chapter Fourteen:
"Out of the Ashes"

Waking up in Vega's arms morning after morning, night after night, day after day, were the most amazing moments of my life. Why? Because of the love that we made? Because of the way he felt? Because of the way he smelt? Because of the way he looked at me? Because of the way I felt when I was with him? Because of his kiss? Because of his voice? Because of the way he knew me? Yes, yes, a thousand times, yes!

It was more than intoxication… it was more than being under his spell… it was more than attraction… it was more than lust… it was love! I loved him! And he loved me! It was as if we were one and the same – intertwined and inseparable from one another.

And yet, I couldn't stop thinking about Melissa. I tried to reach out to her within my mind many times, while I was with Vega and staying in his home – however, each time I did I didn't receive any kind of response. I was beginning to fear the worst – after all I had no idea where she was, nor who she was with.

I knew that Vega could feel how worried I was about Melissa; however, every time I brought up my concerns and my fear about what she may be going through, Vega always assured me by saying:

"Don't worry, Olivia – I will return her to you, even if it is the last thing that I do!"

And I believed him every time that he said that to me.

I loved being with Vega more than anything – but I would be lying if I said that I did not also have other things on my mind when I was with him. Namely: What I was going to do next? Where I was going to go next? I didn't even have a house to go back to, even if I wanted to – because it had been burned to the ground before my eyes? I didn't have anything to wear. I didn't even have a phone – however, Vega did allow me to use his mobile-phone to call into work and inform them that I wouldn't be coming in.

"Why? Because my house burnt down and in the process I lost all of my worldly-possessions" – I explained to them on the phone.

I probably should have called Melissa's school and explained why she had not attended in over a month – but, firstly, I didn't know their number, and secondly, and most importantly, informing them was not a high-priority of mine. No doubt, I would be in a lot of trouble with the education department when they caught up with me – however, like I said, that was not a priority for me at the time.

There was also the matter of the aforementioned arson of my house? My escape from hospital? My assault on that Nurse? Nurse? Nurse? Nurse Jones? But, to be honest, I did not give those potential problems a second thought. All I knew was that I had to keep going – and above else get Melissa back, by any means necessary.

After spending nearly a week with Vega, I couldn't wait any longer – and I asked him again to help me get Melissa back sooner rather than later.

"Vega, please – I need to get Melissa back! If you know where she might be, then please help me get her back?" I asked, as I looked out of Vega's bedroom window and up at the night-sky and to the constellation of Orion, wearing nothing but my underwear – as Vega stood behind me, wearing his red satin robe, with his hands around my waist and his head upon the right-hand-side of my neck.

Knowing that he was a vampire, I did secretly wonder whether he had ever fantasized about sinking his teeth into my neck and sucking the blood out of my carotid artery.

"Olivia, you know that I… that we need to keep a low-profile? As I explained to you, the rebels believe that we are both dead – and I would like to keep it that way for a little while longer, while I plan my next move. I am waiting for Vincent, Val, and the others to make their next move – before I do anything. You see, they are playing a game – but they do not know what they are playing for, nor who they are playing against. If only the rebels had read my books – then they might have a fighting chance at defeating me?"

Said Vega, as I felt his cool breath against my skin – which instantly made the hairs on the back of my neck stand on-end.

"What do you mean?" I asked, as I continued to look out the window at the stars above in the night-sky.

"You've read my books?" Asked Vega.

"Uh-huh! All of them – over and over, many times!" I replied immediately.

"Well, then you already know that the only way to defeat and kill an undying vampire is not to stab him, not to burn him – no, the best way to kill an undying vampire is to capture his heart and steal it away, and then put it in a place where he could never find it. And that is why they wanted you... that is why they have your daughter – because you had my heart from the instant that I saw you. And your daughter? Well, let's just say that she fell in with the wrong crowd – and now that they believe that you are dead, I believe that they will seek to use her gifts to their advantage?" Said Vega – to whom I listened intently to, because I was instantly intrigued by his mentioning of Melissa's "gifts"... only one of which I had an inclination about: her gift of telepathy? But as for having any further knowledge about any other "gifts" that Melissa might have, I was completely in the dark.

However, it seemed, from what Vega was saying at least, that he knew more about Melissa than I did these days.

"Gifts?" I asked; "What gifts?"

"Oh, Olivia – you must know?" Replied Vega, as he began to kiss my neck on both sides.

"Know what? I have no idea what... what... what you are saying?" I replied, awkwardly – as I was simultaneously being seduced by Vega and his lips.

"Like mother, like daughter!" Replied Vega, as he leaned against my right-ear and whispered into it.

"I... I..." I said, as I struggled to find any coherent words at all – because my mind was in another place entirely at that moment.

"She is the offspring of two werewolves, after all – how could she not follow in your paw-prints? So to speak?" Said Vega, as he continued to repeatedly kiss my neck again.

95

However, yet again, something inside me was willing me to call into question what Vega had just said – especially the part about Melissa being "the offspring of two werewolves".

And it was then that I thought to myself: *Wait a minute, how does he know about Alex? Alex – my ex-boyfriend, who I accidentally changed into a werewolf when I scratched him on the back when we were having sex, and the same person who became a pawn of Mingan – Tala's ex – and who subsequently raped me while we were still in our Wolf-forms... which resulted in me becoming pregnant with Melissa, my daughter – who everybody always seems to want to use to further their own agendas.*

"What do you mean? And, while we're at it – how the hell do you know about Alex?" I asked, angrily – as I broke free of Vega's embrace and I looked him straight in the eye.

Vega just stood there, as if in a state of utter surprise at my actions and at the questions that I was asking him.

"Olivia? Olivia? You and I... we... we have made love to each other, over and over again, many times now – do you think that we would not have shared more with each other than our bodies alone? We have been communicating with one-another and sharing each-other's thoughts for a long time – perhaps longer than you may realize? I... I know a great deal about you and your life, and about all that you have been through... thanks to our shared bond. I have seen your memories... I have felt your inner-most feelings... I know every chapter, every line, every life-changing moment that you have had to live through during the story of the Wolf and you, and your shared existence with one-another. I actually find your relationship, your metamorphosis, and your unbreakable and indomitable spirits fascinating, not to mention inspiring!" Said Vega with smile, as he looked at me with a look of glee in his eyes.

I began to cry. I felt so heartbroken in that moment, as I looked into his sparkling eyes.

"How long? How long have you known about... about the Wolf in Me... the Wolf and Me?" I asked, as I stood there heartbroken and aggravated also – because I considered Vega's unsanctioned reading of my thoughts and memories as a violation, and one that I truly did not know how to respond to.

"Olivia, I knew… I knew that there was something special about you from the moment that I saw you. And, in truth, I had been having dreams and premonitions about you for months – long before you and I have even met! I just knew… I knew that you were going to be at that bookstore on that day – and meeting you was the one and only reason that that fake book-signing event was even organized in the first place? Because, as you know, up until that day no one knew who *Vega* was, nor what they looked like! Everything was planned so that I could meet you, and so that you could meet me! And now here we arc! Lovers – in every sense of the word!"

"Did you? Did you do all this? Did you? Did you set all this up? Did you? Did you start a war with your people? Did you instigate this rebellion against yourself? Did you get my daughter kidnapped? Did you nearly get us both killed? Did you do it all, just so that we could be together? Just so that we could stay in your house and make love to each other? Huh? Did you? Have you been manipulating people – me included – just so that you could get me here: exactly where you have always wanted me? Tell me the truth?!?" I screamed, as tears rolled down my cheeks.

Vega said nothing. Why? Because he knew. He knew that I had caught him in the act and I had revealed his true intentions.

And then, after a few seconds of awkward silence, Vega looked at me, and he said:

"Olivia, I love you! You know that I would never do anything to hurt you?" – And I knew that was as close to an admission of guilt as I was ever going to get out of him.

"You bastard!" I shouted.

"Olivia, please – don't do this?" He said.

"Do what?" I screamed at the top of my lungs.

"Olivia, everything will be alright – believe me?"

"Believe you? Believe you? After what you've done? I'll likely never believe another word that comes out of your mouth ever again! You used me? You used Melissa? You knew exactly what was going to happen? And since you know that you are to some degree immortal – you know that no matter how many times they try and kill you, you will always come back! Dracula has nothing on you! Bram Stoker would be loving every moment of this if they were here instead of me – and to them you would no doubt be a gold-mine of vampiric-inspiration! It's also a good job that we are not in one of Anne Rice's books right now either – because I am certain that you and Lestat would have a field-day with one-another, as you decided amongst yourselves who was the best vampire of them all? But, do you know what? This is real! You are who and what you are, and I am who and what I am – so, if you value your life at all and you do not want to put your immortality any further to the test, I'd advise you to answer every one of my questions: firstly, where is Melissa? And don't tell me that you don't know, because I don't believe you! You are the king of the Vampires? You are their god? You know all – and you know what to do, and when to do it? So, just tell me right now: where is my daughter?"

"I don't know, Olivia! You have got to believe me? I truly do not know! But... but I can help you find her? I want... I want to help you to find her?" Replied Vega – with what looked like an expression of sadness on his face.

I was so angry! So angry! I wanted to turn into the Wolf right that second and attack Vega – but... but I didn't... I controlled myself, and I used the anger that I was feeling to clear my mind and allow myself to make clearer choices and decisions about what I was going to do next.

"Ok, let's start with a name?" I asked, as I stared Vega in the eye and I crossed my arms out in front of me.

"A name?" Vega replied, as if he was confused by the question that I had just asked him.

"Yep, a name! The name of the law firm that Val works for? You said that she was a lawyer? Or, at least that was what I heard you say when I was out of my body and listening to the conversation that you were having with the rebels in my house – before it was set a light?" I said, as I got up close to Vega – so close that I hoped he could see in my eyes and on my face that I was not messing around any longer.

"What to do intend to do?" Asked Vega with a look of intrigue on his face.

"I am going to do what we wolves do best: I am going to go for a hunt, and Val is going to be my unwitting prey. And I am going to hunt her and follow her every move until she leads me to wherever the rebel vampires are holding Melissa hostage!" I said in what I hoped was a tone of unwavering determination.

"And what are you going to do when you find the rebels?" Asked Vega; "Just out of interest?"

"Look, all I want is my daughter back! I nearly lost her before, a long time ago – but I am not going to let that happen again! She is my world! She means everything to me! We have been through a lot together! Melissa is all I have – and I will do whatever I have to do to get her back! Now, you can either help me – or not? It's totally up to you? You give me the name of Val's law firm… you let me walk out of here… you let me try and save my daughter – and maybe then I will try and forgive you for what you have done! But, if you try to stand in my way, then you are going to have a fight on your hands – and I am telling you now that you will lose! So, what's it going to be, V? You say that you love me? Ok then, prove it: give me a name?" I asked again, as I stared Vega in the eye unflinchingly – until he started to smile again and he nodded his head up and down, and then he said:

"Ventura & Valance: that is the law firm that Val, or should I say that is the law firm that Valkyrie Sherlock – as she is legally known – works for… for now, at least! Val was always loyal – however, she was also always weak when it came to knowing what ideology to follow and when. She is cunning, adaptive, suspicious, smart, and she has an impressive gift at winning any and every fight that she is faced with – in court, as well as in a physical altercation. She may see you coming before you realize that she knows you are there? But, if you are as good of a hunter as would like me to believe, then I have faith that she will lead you to Melissa. I don't know who else is a part of this rebellion – however, Vincent… Vincent Banks… he appears to have taken the lead in attempting to grab the throne, as it were. Val will lead you to Vincent – and he will lead you to your daughter," said Vega with a forlorn expression on his face.

99

"Thank you!" I said, as I looked him in the eye – before I stepped back and away from Vega.

"I'm sorry – but I cannot go with you. I must remain where I am for the time being: dead, for all intents and purposes… and in the shadows. However, I will attempt to help you whenever and wherever I can – should you need my help?" Replied Vega apologetically.

"That's fine!" I replied immediately, as I stood with my back against the towering window of Vega's bedroom. "But, for right now, I need two things from you? Actually, make that three things?" I said, as I looked at Vega intently.

"And what would they be, may I ask?" Asked Vega with a slight upwards tilt of the head, as he continued to stare at me.

"I want some clothes. I want a car. And I want a place to stay. I want to be out of here by sunrise, and I want to start hunting Val as soon as possible!" I replied forthrightly.

"Olivia, I… It is the middle of the night? Surely all this can wait until tomorrow?" Asked Vega.

"No! No, it can't! Because I have been sitting on my hands for too long now – while god knows what has been happening to Melissa? And I do not want to waste another second in my pursuit of getting her back. So, can you get me what I want?" I asked – with my hands firmly placed upon my hips – as I glared at Vega.

"I… I… I'm sure that all those things can be arranged," replied Vega in a downbeat tone of voice. "Can you give me an hour to get you some clothes? Can you give me two hours to have a car waiting for you outside? And, can you give me until sunrise to have an apartment ready and waiting for you to use, for whenever and for however long you need to use it?" Asked Vega, as he returned my intense stare.

"That… that sounds agreeable!" I replied. "But, for right now, if you need me, I'll be in the bathroom taking a shower! And, before you ask – no, that wasn't an invitation for you to join me! I think, for the time being, that you and I need to keep our relationship strictly business? Ok?" I said, as I stepped forwards again.

"As you wish, Olivia! As I said, I will help you in any way that I can!" Replied Vega, as he watched me walk right passed him – until I was in the corridor outside his bedroom.

I then made my way to the nearby bathroom – the same one that I had used every day I had been staying with Vega.

And as soon as I reached the large red and black decorated bathroom, I quickly undressed... I stepped into the large glass shower-compartment... I turned on the hot water... and as I stood underneath the waterfall of water-droplets, I prepared myself in my mind for what I was going to do next and where I was going to go.

When sunrise arrived, I discovered that Vega really was a man of his word: because waiting outside his house for me was a very sporty-looking red Mercedes-Benz – which had doors on both sides that opened upwards, like the Delorean time-machine from *Back to the Future*. I immediately opened the driver's side door, I stepped inside, and then I sat in the driver's seat. I was now wearing the black jeans, the white t-shirt, the black leather-jacket, and the leather boots that had been procured for me. I was holding the keys to the red Mercedes-Benz that I was now sitting in the drivers-seat of, as well as the keys to the apartment in Birmingham that had also been arranged for me, firmly in my right-hand. In my left-hand-side jacket-pocket I had a new mobile-phone that Vega had given to me – which he told me I could use to get in touch with him at any and every hour of the day.

When I was sitting in the very futuristic-looking Mercedes-Benz – which had a black, red, and silver interior – I must admit that it did take me a minute to figure out how to start it; however, when I saw the Push to Start button I wasted no time in pushing it and starting the car's engine, and then pushing down on the accelerator and hearing the roar of the car's engine. I felt like I was sitting in a sports-car – probably because that was exactly what I was doing.

I wasted no time in driving away from Vega's mansion-home, without looking back, and making my way to the City of Birmingham – with conviction and determination in my heart, knowing that I was one step closer to getting Melissa back.

Chapter Fifteen:
"R&R"

After finally reaching the apartment that Vega had arranged for me – a very spacious and neutral-colored fourth-floor apartment, overlooking a nearby canal basin – I immediately discovered that it had been decorated to a high-spec, and the cupboards and fridge-freezer had been stocked with all manner of food and beverages that instantly caught my eye and appealed to my palette.

Within the closets and the wardrobes of the main bedroom of the apartment there was an assorted collection of items of clothing that all looked as though they would fit me perfectly.

On the double-bed of the main bedroom there lay a dark-brown leather satchel and a large brown envelope with my name on it waiting for me. Inside the satchel there was all manner of pieces of paper – including information regarding the rebels that Vega believed may be a part of the rebellion against him: names, addresses, locations of interest, which all looked to have been handwritten in Vega's own handwriting – as well as a small white envelope with *"To Olivia"* written on it.

I put the leather satchel and its contents aside, and then I reached for the large brown envelope – which had, to my astonishment, thousands of pounds in every kind of denomination of Bank of England notes in it. Suffices to say, there was more money in that envelope than I had ever seen in my life – so much so that I was almost afraid to touch it.

In the main bedroom, opposite the window that lead to a terrace, there was a desk with a laptop on it, next to a fancy chrome-looking metal-lamp, and a telephone with an illuminated large colour screen. On the wall opposite the bed there was a large flat-screen T.V. that looked so thin that you could almost mistake it for a dark mirror, or a part of the wall itself that it was attached to.

The main bedroom, and the whole apartment, was nice, light, and welcoming – however, it was... it was definitely lacking in something. It felt more like an apartment that you would show to potential apartment owners – at least that was the way that it felt to me at first.

After driving for most of the early morning, and then taking quite some time in finding my new apartment – not to mention not getting much sleep the night before – I must admit to having felt greatly exhausted, and in need of some R&R before I proceeded on my hunt. So, with that in mind, I laid down on my new bed, still fully-clothed from head to toe – just planning to have a couple of minutes of laying down with my eyes closed; however, a couple of minutes quickly turned into a couple hours... during which I dreamed.

I dreamed, among other things, that Vega, Melissa, and I, were watching the film '*Back to the Future*' – as we all sat on the sofa, in the living room of our old house, watching one of my favourite movies – until there was a sudden knock on the front-door. In my dream, I remember standing up from the sofa, walking over to the front-door, opening it – and then revealing that it was in fact Tala who was standing on the other side of the door, with a smile on her face, and carrying an electric torch in her right-hand which she immediately shined into my eyes, as she said:

"*See the light! See the light!*" over and over again – before she spontaneously combusted into a plume of black smoke.

The next part of my dream featured Vega running through a forest, at night, and seemingly being chased by ominous anthropomorphic shadows that looked like rampant creatures – from where I was observing them, anyway. And I also dreamed that Melissa was in a hospital, wearing a hospital gown, and about to give birth – but, in my dream, she died in childbirth after delivering a blood-soaked wolf-cub.

My dreams were... they were surreal, to say the least – and for a few moments there, while I was dreaming, I actually believed that everything I saw was in fact real. However, fortunately, it was all a dream – and when I awoke from that horrendous nightmare, I decided to waste no time in getting up, venturing out of my new apartment, and then making my way into Birmingham City centre.

As I walked along the canal-way, I did a quick Google search on my phone for the exact location of the law firm where Val worked – which I discovered was located on Cherry Street. I also knew that, no matter what I did, I needed to not attract too much attention to myself – nor look, or sound, suspicious in any way, as I tried to track down Val and follow her every move.

Chapter Sixteen:
"The Hunt"

One of the things that I have learned over the years is this: if you want to be a good and an effective hunter – while hunting for anything, or for anyone – you first need to master the art of patience, and also the art of being ambivalent to what time of the day it is. Whether it is morning, noon, or night, a hunt is a hunt, and it can last for a minute, an hour, a day – but, no matter how long it takes and where it takes you, you cannot for a second give up on catching your prey.

With that in mind, I exercised the art of patience as best as I could in my hunt for Val, as I waited, as I watched, and as I learned as much as I could about the law firm that she worked for, over the next couple of days after I moved into my new apartment – which I was now using as my make-shift base of operations and where I would return to day after day and plan the next phases of my hunt.

Fortunately, there was a Starbucks coffee-shop directly opposite the office building in which *Ventura & Valance* was located – so I spent most of my time looking out of the window at the law firm, and at the people who came and went through its revolving glass door.

As I waited, and as I observed, I consumed a great deal of food – not to mention caffeine; however, I did not just eat and drink, as I waited for a glimpse of Val, I also made notes in a notebook that I bought from a nearby stationery store which I filled with times, descriptions, and routines that I observed. I sat in the Starbucks for so long, day-after-day, that I naturally got asked by the baristas who worked in the coffee-shop: *"what are you writing?"* And I always replied:

"Oh, nothing really! Just the story of my life!"

I was beginning to believe that I would never actually get to see Val either enter or exit through the revolving-door of the law firm, nor anybody who I would recognize – which was why I was so surprised to see a very familiar face enter the office building of

Ventura & Valance. It was none other than the same snooty familiar face of the man that I still remembered seeing after I woke up in Vega's bed over a month ago – after Vega and I had had that little misunderstanding about what Vega's true intentions were towards me. I was led to believe, at the time, that the man who I spoke to on that morning was merely Vega's assistant? Or perhaps his butler? And that was why I was so surprised that, after all this time, here he was walking into the same offices that I had under observation – and, even then, I knew that his appearance was no mere coincidence.

What are they doing here? I asked myself. *Were they here on behalf of Vega? Or did they have their own reasons for visiting the same law firm that Val worked for?* I didn't think that Vega had sent them here – because, as far as everybody else was concerned, Vega had died in the same house fire that destroyed my home… at least that was what I had been lead to believe? The man did not seem too phased about walking around in broad daylight either – which shocked me, because I had assumed that he was a vampire also?

What is he doing here? I asked myself. *I don't even know his name? But Vega – he must know? Surely? After all, he did work for him?*

However, then it occurred to me: *if Val did not come out, and if I couldn't follow her – perhaps I could follow whatever his name was and see where he went?*

So, I waited… I waited… and I waited – until 5 o'clock that same evening – when the Starbucks that I was in was starting to close, when I had to get up and go outside. And it was then, just as there appeared to be a flood of people leaving their respective businesses and heading home for the day, that I saw Val and the man who used to work for Vega leave *Ventura & Valance* – and holding hands, as they walked away from the office building.

They must be in a relationship with one-another? I thought to myself.

This was when my hunt finally began – and though I tried to maintain an effective distance, without being seen by either Val or her companion, I did get the feeling, as I followed their every move, that they somehow knew that they were being followed? Because they took their time and they did not seem to be in any kind of a hurry to get to anywhere in particular.

It was already 6 o'clock in the evening, and I knew that I had to keep my instincts as sharp as possible at all times in order to not lose my prey – namely the two vampires in front of me.

I followed Val and her companion for miles through the now dark city streets – and then, finally, at about 6.45p.m, I followed them into this bar called *"The Intro Venus", or "The I.V." for short* – the name of which I instantly recognized as being a play on words, because it sounded exactly like the word "intravenous" when you said it quickly.

It was obvious that this place was some kind of "Vampire-bar" – however, when I walked inside, the fact that it was a bar for vampires was not plainly apparent; but, why would it be? It's not as if any normal person would suspect that the red wine that they served in this bar was really blood? Why would they? I don't actually know that they actually sold blood by the bottle, or anything like that – but I don't think that it is too much of a stretch of the imagination to assume, because... because what I witnessed next convinced me beyond any shadow of a doubt that the bar that I had followed Val into was indeed a "Vampire-bar".

I followed Val and her companion through the busy crowd of people, inside the darkly-lit bar, to the very back of the large space – where the entrances to the toilets were located, that had printed on them individually: "Men"... "Women"... "Disabled"... "Staff"... and also a door which had the letter "V" printed upon it in what looked like red paint – and it was that door that Val and her companion entered through. I chose to not immediately follow them through the door with the letter "V" on it – because, quite honestly, at the time, I did not know what lay on the other side.

As the night went on, the lighting in the darkly-lit bar steadily changed to a dark-red hue – as patrons came and went, until there was no more than a handful of people in the bar, one of whom being me. And it was as I sat in one of the booths of the bar that I got the distinct impression that I had potentially walked into a trap, and for all intents and purposes I was now surrounded?

However, I continued to sit and wait – periodically looking around to the door with the letter "V" on it every so often.

I was about to get up and walk out of the bar; however, then I heard a door creak open, and also the sound of foot-falls slowly walking over the floor of the now silent bar – the sounds of which echoed more so now that hardly anybody was in the bar.

And then I heard a voice coming from behind me say my name:

"Olivia Hunter? How nice it is to see you after so long?" Said the snooty voice of Vega's former assistant/butler/whatever.

I slowly turned around in my seat, and then I quickly came face to face with the same vampire who I had met over a month ago in Vega's bedroom – and who I had seen walk into the bar with Val.

"Do you come here often?" Asked the vampire with a smile – wearing a grey-suit with a red handkerchief in the left-hand-side pocket of his jacket, a red-shirt, and a pair of shiny crimson-red leather shoes.

"No!" I replied; "It's… it's my first time, actually! How about you?" I asked with a smile – as I quickly calculated in my mind the potential options that I had available to me: one being, a way out of the bar… in case I needed it.

"Oh yes! All the time, in fact! The 1787 Chateau Margaux is divine! You must try it? How about I get us a couple of glasses?" Said the vampire – with a look in his eye that I could not read accurately; however, at least to me, he looked like he was enjoying every moment.

"I'm fine!" I replied, as I put my right hand into the air. "I was… I was actually just about to leave, as a matter of fact!" I said, as I began to shuffle myself out of the booth where I was sat.

"Not at all! I insist! Just a little sip! And, believe me, you will never forget it!" Said the vampire, as he put his right-hand on my left-hand and he gently held it down upon the table – as he too sat down at the booth.

"Us meeting here is so serendipitous – do you not think? After all this time?" Said the vampire with a grin.

"Of course! Of course! It's just that I… I need to get home! I… I have a lot of work to catch-up on… and it is getting very late?" I said nervously, as I tried to remove my hand from underneath the vampire's ice-cold touch.

"Oh, but you can't, Olivia – not before... not before we become reacquainted with one another? You see, I believe that you and I got off on the wrong foot when we last saw one another. I mean, when you are standing under the shadow cast by someone intimidating – it can be hard to know the right words to say? Yes? Just as when you work for someone without a soul – it can be hard to relearn how to act around other people? Especially women who are as beautiful and lovely as you are?" Said the sniveling vampire.

"That is so sweet of you to say, Mister... Mister?" I replied, as I looked into the vampire's dark eyes.

"Mister? Oh, I am no Mister?" Replied the vampire with a chuckle – before he continued; "However, if you so require, you may call me Vanguard – if you so wish?" Said "Vanguard" with a smile and a quick wink from his right-eye.

"Vanguard, huh?" I replied, as I studied his every movement.

"Yes! In fact, that name was given to me by a mutual acquaintance of ours – a very... very long time ago! They... they gave me that name at the same time that they gave me the place by their side that I enjoyed for so long," replied Vanguard quietly – before one of the bar staff appeared near our booth, holding a wooden tray with a full bottle of a 1787 Chateau Margaux red wine that looked as pristine as it would have done back in the 18th Century when it was originally bottled, as well as two large wine glasses.

The bar-man set both the old bottle of wine, and the two wine glasses down on the table as gently as he could – and then he stepped away and he disappeared from view.

"Here we are! As promised! I know that you will love this!" Said Vanguard, as he proceeded to uncork the old bottle of wine.

"I... I... I really do need to be going?" I said, as I tried to shuffle out of the booth again – however, when I looked towards the entrance of the bar I noticed that there were two men standing by the now closed doors.

"Just have a little taste? This bottle alone is worth more than you could make in a year – maybe even two years at your job as a…?" said Vanguard, as he successfully uncorked the bottle of red wine with a wide-eyed grin. "There!"

"Please, I… I…" I said, as I tried as hard as I could to get myself out of the current predicament that I found myself in.

"Olivia? This won't take long? And I have been saving this very bottle for a very special occasion?" Said Vanguard, as he proceeded to pour the contents of the bottle of wine into the two wine glasses on the table in between us.

And then, when he was done emptying the entirety of the wine bottle into both glasses, Vanguard took a hold of the wine glass directly in front of him and he raised it into the air.

"I… I would like to raise a glass and call a toast? Will you join me, Olivia?" Said Vanguard, as he looked me in the eye – and as he held out his now full wine-glass out in front of him.

I reluctantly reached out for the other glass of wine, and then I too raised it up – and then I said:

"And what is the occasion?" I asked, as I readied myself to call upon the Wolf to break free.

"Why, the death of a god? The death of a dictator! The fall of a king! The king is dead… the king is dead! Long live the king!" Said Vanguard exuberantly, as he reached out and touched his wine glass to mine.

"Who?" I asked nonchalantly.

"Why, the king of us all! Someone… the one we all once loved, worshipped, trusted… the one who we would have continued to have done anything and everything for – however, someone… someone… the one… the one who ultimately betrayed us all! However, he… *they* are now dead – because… because they did not listen! They are dead, because they turned their back on their own kind! They are dead, because their people learned how to live without them! They are dead, because… because of you! Because of you, Olivia Hunter! And that is why you are here!" Said Vanguard – before he took a large gulp of the wine from his glass.

"Ah! Ah, yes! Umm, that is as exquisite as I remember! That is divine! However, not as exquisite, nor as divine, as the blood from the veins of a still beating heart! But what could ever hope to be?" Said Vanguard with a smile.

"I'm not sure whether you are aware of this, but the man... the one who you had sex with... the one who brought you into his home... the one who defied the will and defiled the livelihood of his people... the one who broke your heart and sent you away... the one who went to your house, and who died within it as the flames engulfed him... He... Vega... was a vampire! He was our king! But, now he is dead – and now I am the king! And, if you have not yet guessed, I too am a vampire – as is everybody in this room, as a matter of fact!" Said Vanguard smugly.

"No? Really? Oh my god! You're joking? I can't believe this! Wow! I had no idea! I wasn't expecting that!" I said sarcastically with a smile – before I burst out into a fit of laughter.

"Sorry... sorry, I didn't mean to sound so sarcastic there – but, you know, sometimes that part of me just comes out unexpectedly? And it's not the only thing that does!" I said, as I put down my glass of wine on the table and I moved it to my right-hand-side.

"You already knew all that?" Asked Vanguard with a frown.

Oh dear, I think I just stole his thunder? I sarcastically thought.

"Hmm, let me think? Well, yeah! Yeah, I suppose I did? Call it... call it women's intuition? Call it instinct? Call it... call it: I know a blood-sucker when I'm looking at one? Or, you could call it: Vega told me all this before he... before he died!" I said, as I purposefully hesitated.

"He did? Well, to be honest, I am not at all surprised – after all, he was crazy when the end came for him?" Replied Vanguard with a grin.

"Really? And how would you know that? I don't remember you showing up to my house? And where were you when my house was being torched, by the way? At home? In your coffin, perhaps? Hanging upside down from the ceiling, maybe? Enjoying a glass of be positive, by any chance?" I replied sarcastically – which I realized might not be at all advisable, especially since I could see that Vanguard was beginning to get a little annoyed by me.

"And how is it that you survived, Olivia? And, may I ask, where have you been since the fire at your home?" Asked Vanguard.

"Didn't your mother ever tell you that it is rude to answer a question with a question?" I replied with a smile.

"No! Did yours?" Replied Vanguard immediately – and very annoyed at this point.

"You see, Olivia, nobody has seen you, nor heard anything from you, in quite some time – and people… some people have been worried about your well-being. They… we have all been concerned about what happened to you, and where you went. And, where was it that you went, Olivia?" Replied Vanguard, as he finally put his glass of wine to the side also.

"Oh, somewhere… somewhere far away… somewhere safe!" I replied, as I leaned in towards Vanguard.

"And with whom? May I ask?" Asked Vanguard, as he mirrored my pose and he too leaned in towards me.

"With… with me? Myself? And I? And we had a very good time! And, yeah, you know, that time away was just what I needed! It was just what anybody would need after they witnessed a dozen or so Molotov cocktails being thrown into their home, I would imagine?" I replied sarcastically, as I glared at Vanguard from across the other side on the booth.

And then Vanguard sat quietly for a moment, seemingly smiling to himself – as if he were thinking – and then he said:

"I'm sure! I'm sure! However, you see the thing is – and that which has been preoccupying my mind since I realized that your body had not been recovered from the remains of your house – and what I cannot stop asking myself is: Where did you go? Who helped you get out? And who has been keeping you safe? And, following on from what you have just said, I also have to wonder: How? How? How did you know that your house was set on fire by Molotov cocktails? And I ask that question, because I was lead to believe that you were unconscious at the time that your house was set ablaze? However, it is possible that you were not really unconscious? But, if you had been awake, no doubt you might have died in place of your precious Vega? Because, without question, you would have put yourself within the path of the blade that stabbed our former vampire king through the chest?" Said Vanguard – smiling throughout.

"Well, yes! Yes, you are completely right! I... I was indeed unconscious! But, just because a person is unconscious that does not mean that they are not aware of what is going on around them, in other ways?" I replied with a smirk.

"You know what? Why don't we just cut the crap? And why don't you just tell me how you got out of your house without even a scratch on you?" Asked a very annoyed looking Vanguard.

"Just lucky, I guess? It was... it was a miracle, I tell you!" I replied with a grin.

"You know... I could fly over this table within a split-second and rip your throat open before you could say another word? But, today, I am feeling benevolent? So, instead, I am going to ask you one last time: How did you survive? And, who... who helped you?" Asked Vanguard, as he stood up ever so slightly so that he look down upon me.

And what happened next? Well, you could say that all hell broke loose – because that was when all the lights in the bar suddenly went out, and when the Wolf in Me came out.

Chapter Seventeen:
"Seeing in the dark"

Even in the dark, as the Wolf, I could see Vanguard as clear day standing near the booth which we had both been sitting at – as he was looking around the bar in every direction with his fangs on full-display.

I didn't know at first whether he could see me – however, the more that he walked around the bar, seemingly as if he were reaching out for wherever I was, told me that if he could see anything it wasn't much, if at all?

"Olivia? Olivia? Where are you, Olivia?" Asked Vanguard, as he tentatively walked in the opposite direction to where I was standing. Of course, I was now in my Wolf-form – so I could not communicate with Vanguard directly; however, I continued to listen to what he said.

"You by the door? Find out what happened to the electricity! We must have blown a fuse, or something? Open the front-door at least – perhaps then we can shed some light upon where our new prisoner is?" Shouted Vanguard to the two vampire guards standing near the entrance/exit of the bar.

"Did you hear what I said, Olivia? You are now our prisoner – whether you like it, or not? But this time we won't let you get away – and we won't let you do what your daughter did. But, make no mistake, we made her pay! Just as we will make you pay for what you have done!" Said Vanguard – as I continued to watch him turn around on the spot, as he seemingly waited for my reply.

What did he just say about, Melissa? I'm not sure – but it sounds as if she gave as good as she got while she was being held captive? But, what I still didn't know was where she was? Nor did I know if she was alright? And did he just say that they "made her pay"? I thought to myself.

I almost leaped forwards and attacked Vanguard while he still could not see me – however, when I suddenly heard the sound of the front-doors of the bar unlatch and then open, I decided to take my opportunity to bolt towards the entrance/exit of the bar and knock the two vampires that were guarding it off of their feet, as I left the bar and instantly ran for cover down a nearby alley-way.

Soon after, I hid myself in the shadows – however, still in full-view on "The I.V". I saw both Val and Vanguard run out of the bar and into the street, followed by the vampires who had been guarding the doors, and Vincent also – the vampire who had seemingly led the group of rebel vampires who had broken into my home and set it on fire, almost two weeks before.

"Where is she? How? How could you let her escape?" I heard Vanguard say to the two vampire guards.

"I didn't even see her leave, sir?" Said one of the guards.

"Sir?" Said Vanguard immediately.

"I'm sorry – I mean, your majesty!" Replied the same guard, as he corrected himself.

"And where we you two when I needed you? You must have known what was happening?" Asked Vanguard to both Vincent and Val.

"We were… we were feeding, your majesty! Two homeless men that were picked up the other night, near the Bullring. That is one of the things that you have got to love about these big cities: there are so many people living on the streets, and nobody even misses any one of them when they disappear!" Said Vincent – with what I believed was a perverse look in his eyes, as he described his abduction of two innocent homeless people and the act of feeding upon them as if it were nothing? As if it were an everyday activity?

"I don't care!" Said Vanguard in reply. "All I care about is finding that woman – and also finding out what, or whom, just made all the lights in there go out simultaneously! Just as I… just as I was preparing to feed myself… upon the flesh and blood of that intolerable woman! I don't know what Vega could ever have seen in her?" Said Vanguard, as he looked at Val – as if he expected her to have all the answers.

Maybe it's because I'm awesome? I thought to myself.

"She's different! She is not just any woman – she has gifts, just as her daughter does!" said Val, as she looked around the dark street outside the bar – no doubt in search of me.

"Are you saying that she too… that she can also turn into a Wolf?" Asked Vanguard – and at the same time confirming to me, indirectly, that Melissa had indeed followed in her mother's footsteps and that she had inherited the gift of the Wolf from me.

I knew it! I just knew it! But, how? And why did she seemingly, voluntarily, get into that black Mercedes without any sign of hesitation? Was she coerced, somehow? Threatened?

"I believe so, my king!" Replied Val.

"But, how? And why would Vega choose to associate himself with such a creature? He must have known who, and what, she was before he… before he invited her back to his home to share his bed?" Said Vanguard, as he too looked for any sign of me in the shadows of the surrounding street.

"Do you think that somebody has been helping her?" Asked Val.

"They must be – how else would she have gotten out of that burning house? You did say that she was unconscious when you left them both?" Asked Vanguard to Val.

"She was – I swear, my king!" Replied Val without hesitation.

"And you are sure that He… that He was dead when you last saw him? This could not be… Him, could it?" Asked Vanguard with touch of urgency in his voice.

"I swear to you, your majesty – the king… I mean *Vega*… he was dead! He is dead! I killed him with my own two hands! I used a shard of black-glass – the same one that you gave to me?" Replied Vincent immediately.

"But?" Said Val, as she began to speak – before she stopped herself.

"But what? Speak up, Val?" Said Vanguard, as he stared intently at her.

"Vincent… he… you did not allow us to feed upon him? So we do not know what happened after we left the house? Perhaps? He? Perhaps, He?" Said Val – almost nervously – as she looked from Vanguard to Vincent and then back again to Vanguard.

"No! No! It can't be! It can't be him! He died! You saw his body with your own eyes?" Said Vincent defensively.

"Yes! Yes, I saw his body! But, how else do you think she got out? She must have had help? And the only other person within the vicinity was Vega!" Said Val, as she made a very logical deduction as to how I got out of my house as it burned around me – and she was spot-one in her assertion.

It was in that moment that I understood why Vega had warned me about Val and about her abilities.

I thought for sure that my hiding place would soon be discovered, and I would have to make a run for it – however, for all the time that I remained hidden, nobody made so much as a move to investigate the surrounding area.

"Your majesty, I state my life on the fact that Vega is dead – and no matter what anybody says, He is not coming back!" Asserted Vincent - however, inaccurately.

"I will hold you to that!" Said Vanguard, as he stared directly into Vincent's eyes.

"In any case, we need to get off the street before we attract any further attention to ourselves?" Said Val, as she took a hold of Vanguard's right-forearm with her left-hand – however, she then quickly removed it when she noticed that Vincent was staring at her.

What is this? Is there some kind of Vampire love-triangle going on? Give me a break! I thought to myself.

"Yes, of course – but tomorrow… tomorrow I want a group to head Vega's old mansion and see if they can detect anything there that might seem out of the ordinary. As far as I am aware nobody has been there since the night he died? So no one should have been there in the intervening time? I will meet them there at some point tomorrow evening, so that I may see whether I can ascertain if anything seems out of the ordinary – just in case you are wrong, Vincent? However, for your sake, I hope you are not!" Said Vanguard, as he looked both Val and Vincent in the eye individually.

"Yes, your majesty!" Said Val, as she returned Vanguard's gaze; however, she then gave Vincent a slight side-glance – which told me, even from where I was, that those two had something to talk about between themselves.

And then, Val, Vincent, and Vanguard, all turned around and went back inside *"The Intro Venus"*, followed afterwards by the two ineffective guards.

I stayed lying low in the dark alley-way – where I remained for a considerable amount of time after the vampires had disappeared from view – as I counted my blessings, and as I planned in my mind what I was going to do when I returned to my human-form. However, due to the fact that I had changed into the Wolf when I was in the bar, I was now without any clothes to change back into when I changed back into my human-form – which left me with no other choice but to try and make my way back to my apartment as the Wolf and then change back into Olivia once I got there.

Fortunately, I had not brought my mobile-phone with me, nor any keys that I would need to get back into my apartment – however, I knew that I had conveniently left a spare-key under the "WELCOME HOME" mat that lay in the hallway outside the front-door of my apartment. What can I say? Hiding stuff – keys, clothes, the truth, the fact that I am a werewolf – comes naturally to me… as does planning for any and every eventuality. In my own personal vocabulary, Hiding was just another word for Surviving.

So, I went home – and I tried to move as quickly as I could through the darkness of the night without a member of the public seeing me.

Chapter Eighteen:
"I spoke too soon"

The next morning – after I finally returned to my apartment, and I managed to change back into my human-form, retrieve the spare-key that I had left for myself to find from underneath the WELCOME HOME doormat, and then successfully open the front-door without being seen, and without any clothes on – I woke up in bed, still naked from the night before… and, as the band *Duran Duran* would say, I was: *"Hungry like a wolf"!* I was hungry for something to eat – as well as hungry for information.

The night before, after I walked into my apartment, I remember being incredibly tired – however, I did have just enough energy in me to find the mobile-phone that Vega had given me, so that I could message him that the rebel vampires – led by none other than Vanguard – were going to be paying his house a visit. I told Vega that if he wanted to stay dead, then he might want to leave while he could and get somewhere safe. However, when I picked up the mobile-phone again, to see if I had received a reply from Vega, there was no message notifications to be found – so I was in the dark at that point about whether he knew who was on their way.

When I woke up, it was already 11 o'clock in the morning – and outside my bedroom window the sun was already shining brightly and streaming in to fill the room with sunlight.

A day like today must be hell for vampires? Knowing how much they hate ultraviolet light? I thought to myself, as I looked to the un-curtained window with a smile on my face.

I was lucky to get out of that vampire bar in one piece last night – I thought, as I replayed in my mind the events that took place the previous evening.

But, it looks like Vega's plan – whatever that is – is going the way he wants it to? Because, by all accounts, the other vampires still think that he is dead? Well, at least that vampire "Vincent" believes he is – even though I think Vanguard and Val are beginning to suspect otherwise? Maybe they know Vega better than he thinks they do? Maybe they expect him to still be alive?

And after all that happened last night, what do I know about where Melissa is? And if she is still alive? Well, I know that she has the Wolf inside her? And I know that she has changed into the Wolf on more than one occasion – that much is clear? And she has also being putting up quite a fight against her captives – which pleases me no end. But, where is she?

I suppose I could have hung around that vampire bar a little longer last night and continued my hunt? But had I done so there is no telling if I would have got any closer to finding out where Melissa is? For all I know, she could be thousands of miles away by now? She could be comatose? She could be? She could be?

I was relieved – however, I was also frustrated, to say the least.

I had this horrible fear that if I did not find Melissa soon, then I might never find her. And I could not stop myself from feeling guilty... guilty about drawing Melissa into whatever had happened/what was happening with Vega and I – which, in all honesty, I was still none the wiser about at this point?

I kept asking myself: *Did Vega's people – the other vampires – really rebel against him because of me? Because he fell in love with me? Really? Was that all it took to dethrone him so quickly? To kill him? And, if so, then why? Why? Because I'm a werewolf, and not a vampire? They can't tell me that no other vampire has ever fell in love with a human man or woman before? They can't say that vampire's don't regularly have sex with humans? Of course they do! I mean, they probably sink their teeth into the necks of their victims after they have slept with them – so it can't be that out of the ordinary? Maybe all the fuss came about because Vega was like a god to them? Maybe he still is? I mean, he's not really dead – he's still walking around, as far as I'm aware? He isn't just any vampire, though – even I can tell that? I don't think there are that many vampires who have the gift of resurrection? Nor the ability to walk around in someone's mind and experience their memories, as Vega had admitted to have done with mine?*

However, I had no idea what Vega's endgame was, nor what he was doing at that very moment. But what I did know for certain was that I had to get in touch with him before I made my next move, because my options at that point seemed even more limited than they had before?

As I continued to lie in bed, I decided to turn on the T.V. for some background noise – while I continued to think about Melissa, about Vega, and about my life as it was – and I did not plan to pay that much attention to what was being shown on the television; however, when I heard the words *"wolf"* and *"captured"* my attention was instantly drawn to the T.V. screen on the wall opposite to where I was lying on the bed.

And then, I saw it: there, on the T.V. screen, I saw the Wolf – I saw myself, as a matter of fact: captured within a grainy-looking photograph, that apparently someone had taken of a wolf/me when they were making their way home after a night-out. Apparently, the man who reportedly saw the wolf/me and took a picture of them/me was *"so scared out of their wits"* that they *"feared that they were going to be eaten alive"*?

Eaten alive? Please! I might be a wolf sometimes – but I do have standards when it comes to what, or who I decide to eat?

The image of me that had been captured was grainy and slightly blurry, but it was definitely a photograph of a wolf – and it was definitely of me, as I ran up Broad Street, before I made my way down the toe-path of the canal towards my apartment building.

So much for me not being spotted by a member of the public? I thought. *But, not to worry – at least I didn't really attack anyone? I might have scared this poor man half-to-death, but at least I didn't eat him!*

They even interviewed a Police Superintendent on the news, and he told the reporter interviewing him that they *"were investigating this potential sighting of a wolf"*, and that they *"were taking the matter very seriously"*, and *"if anybody else was an eye-witness to the wolf in question"* then they should call a phone number on the screen and *"someone would visit them and interview them regarding what they saw"*.

Yes, because a lone wolf in a city is something to worry about? Not a secret society of vampires who were abducting people, drinking blood, and staging a coup against their king? No – because that would be something unbelievable, right? Downright unheard of, correct? And nothing to worry about? But, a lone wolf? Oh yes, get on that straight away! I'll probably be a headline on a newspaper by this time tomorrow? BEWARE! FEROCIOUS, BLOOD-THIRSTY, WOLF ON THE PROWL AND ON THE STREETS OF BIRMINGHAM! DON'T GO OUT AFTER DARK – ESPECIALLY NOT WHEN THERE IS A FULL-MOON! I can see it now – that headline, along with that blurry and grainy picture of me running down Broad Street? Great! – I sarcastically thought.

And I was just about to start imagining another headline, and another story being reported about me – when my mobile-phone suddenly began to ring, and when I looked at the screen I saw that it was Vega who was calling me.

"Hello, this is Olivia Hunter – how may I direct your call?" I said, as I answered the phone to Vega.

"Olivia? Olivia, I need to see you! I need you to meet me?" Said Vega – sounding a little exasperated.

"Why?" I asked, as I sat up on the bed; "What's happened?"

"It's... it's your daughter... they... I know where they have her!" Said Vega.

"Melissa?" I replied immediately; "You mean she's still alive? Where? Where is she?" I asked, as I jumped out of the bed and I immediately started to get dressed into some clothes – however, while continuing to keep the phone as close to my ear as possible so that I did not miss a word that Vega said.

"Just meet me at my home – I will be waiting for you near the main gate at 10 p.m." said Vega.

"Why? What aren't you telling me? And, if time is of the essence, then why wait until 10 o'clock tonight? Why don't we just find whoever is holding Melissa and make them take us to her?" I replied – stressing out about what Vega had just said, as well as being a tad annoyed by his lack of immediacy.

"No, Olivia! If we do something now, then we may accidentally tip off the rebels that we are coming?" Replied Vega – annoyingly nonchalant about the whole thing.

"Vega, this is my daughter we're talking about! If she's in danger, then we need to get her back now! And why wait till 10 o'clock? I don't understand? And why do we have to meet at your house? What's happened? What do you know?" I asked, as I collected all of my things together – my keys, my purse, my notebook – and I threw them all into my shoulder bag, and then I quickly put on my black leather-jacket, and my boots, and I walked towards the front door of the apartment.

"Olivia, this is the only way to save my race! My children! I cannot let Vanguard plunge the entire world into a state of war – and a war that would ultimately draw all of humanity into it also? He... Vanguard seeks to bring us out of the shadows and establish us – vampires – as a recognized race in our own right? He wants us to have our own country? Our own laws? Our own weapons? Vanguard seeks the annihilation of the rest of humanity! He seeks to burn this world to the ground, so that he can rise from the ashes and become the sole ruler of this planet!" Said Vega.

By this time, I was already out of my apartment and making my way to the red Mercedes that was parked in a nearby parking bay.

"Look, Vega – I get that Vanguard... I get that he is crazy, and that he wants to be the king of the vampires? But... but world-domination? Where has all that come from? Why? Why now? And how does he think the rest of the world will react to the news that a terrorist is seeking to over-throw all the governments of the world? And, how does he expect to be able to do that? He is just one vampire – with definite delusions of grandeur – who is leading a band of rebels, who seem just as weak-minded as he does?" I asked.

"Olivia, vampires are everywhere! We are already in every country on this planet – and now that I am dead, or at least believed to be, this is when Vanguard will instigate his grand idea of Vampire dominion. Well, when I say "his grand idea" – I also mean mine... at least, it was something that I pondered centuries

ago? However, I am not the same vampire that I once was! I changed! I loved! I lost! I lead my people down a better path! I met people! I met you! And when I did meet you, I changed again! And Vanguard, he knew this also? He too saw the change in me? And he knew that I had spoken of my belief that you and I had met each other before – in another life, maybe? I don't know how long he has been planning all this, but I know that he intends to use you daughter as a sacrifice?" Said Vega.

By this time, I was in the driver's seat of the red Mercedes and driving as fast as I could through the city – all the while crying tears from both eyes.

"I'm on my way to your house right now!" I sobbed down the phone to Vega.

"No, Olivia – you can't!" Replied Vega immediately.

"You wanna' bet? I'm not letting that vampire scum sacrifice my daughter for anything – you got that?" I screamed down the phone.

"But, this is not the time! How do you know that Melissa will be with them when they are at my house?" Asked Vega.

And that was when the penny dropped – as they say – and I had a very bizarre thought, which I expressed verbally to Vega at the same time that I was thinking it.

"Because… because Melissa has been right under our noses the entire time? Your mansion? That's where she is! That's where she has been this entire time!" I shouted, as I felt like I was having a moment of revelation.

"Impossible!" Vega replied immediately; *"If she were at my home, then I would have known – as would you have?"* Said Vega.

And he was right.

"But… but… that is where she is! That thing is massive! Your house is vast, and it has acres of ground? You said it yourself, a while ago: there used to be another structure where your house now stands, right? Tell me, what used to be there?" I asked, as I had a flash-back in my mind to the first time that I visited Vega's house.

"A crossroads? An opening between worlds? A gateway to a place where vampires were once born – where I was conceived… where I was left… and where I was found! And the place where I

entered this world, and where I gave birth to my people! Where I became a god to my people! The place where my home now stands was once – and still is – the one place on Earth where other dimensions of space and time can be traversed!" Said Vega – sounding as if he was getting emotional on the other end of the phone.

"What do you mean? I don't understand?" I asked – because what he was saying did not make any sense to me, at the time.

"Other dimensions, Olivia! Alternate universes! There are other worlds that exist besides this one – all existing in the same place, at the same time, but on different planes of perception! I have visited such worlds! I... I came from such a world! A world where there were two dominant races on this planet – Vampires and Humans – who were constantly at war with one-another! A world where humanity decimated and slaughtered almost every last vampire in existence – all but one: me! I found the place where my house now stands when I was a child, but in another dimension of existence: a place where there was a tear in the fabric of reality that I used to come and go through, as I visited one different universe after another!" Explained Vega – as my head felt like it was on the verge of exploding as a result of this information overload that Vega was giving me.

"So, what? You're... you're from another universe? Another universe where there was once a race of vampires that... what? Had their own countries? Their own customs? Their own language?" I asked – though, admittedly, not knowing exactly what I was asking.

"Yes!" Replied Vega without hesitation.

"I was the offspring of Marcus and Melis! And I am the only living heir to the throne of the Vampire Royal Family!" Said Vega.

"But, hang on a minute – you said that you were immortal? You said, and I saw, that you cannot die? How? How is that possible? Because, I'm guessing that all the other vampires on this planet are not like you, and they are susceptible to things like sunlight? Stakes through the heart? You know, that kind of thing?" I asked – as I simultaneously attempted to drive as fast as I could without being pulled over by the police for speeding.

"I'm special, Olivia! I don't know what else to say? But, I do know that I have a power within me: a spirit that will not let me die? And you know what that is like? To have this phenomenal energy inside you? This indomitable spirit that keeps you going? Don't you, Olivia? The wolf in you – they know what I am talking about?" Said Vega – as he spoke to a deeper part of my soul than I could ever possibly describe.

"Are you some kind of Vampires Messiah, or something?" I asked.

"Perhaps I am, Olivia! At least that has always been my belief? And now I must save my people from those who seek to destroy them! Vincent? Val? Vanguard? They do not know what path they are walking down?" Said Vega.

"How? How did you find out what they intend to do? And why? Why do they think they need to sacrifice Melissa?" I asked, as I raced towards the countryside and to where I knew Vega's mansion was located.

"Because, like you, Melissa is a werewolf? And, because, like you, Melissa will not give up – unless she loses that which matters the most to her: her mother! Sacrifice has long been an important symbol in Vampire society – and the sacrifice of a werewolf, to the rebels, and to the entire world of Vampires, would be like the lighting of a fuse!" Said Vega.

"Which is why we need to stop them!" I shouted down the phone, as I held it in my right-hand; "Which is why I believe… which is why I know she is there! At your home! I'm sure of it!" I said – completely and utterly convinced that my instincts were right.

"How can you be sure?" Asked Vega.

"Because I am Melissa's mother – and your mother was called "Melis", you said? Which sounds a lot like Melissa, don't you think? So, yeah – there's that! And, you know what? I don't believe in coincidences? I instead believe that everything happens for a reason! And I believe that I am going to save Melissa – even if I have to sacrifice my own life in the process?" I said, as I began to cry again.

"Olivia, I... I don't know what to say?" Said Vega – sounding uncharacteristically lost for words.

"Vega, I am telling you – she is there! At your home! And Vanguard has been keeping her prisoner, right under your nose, since he arranged for her to be kidnapped? And why? Why do you think he did that? Because of us! Because of me! Because he wanted to use Melissa to get to me, and because he wanted to use me to get to you!" I said.

"I... I... I think you are right, Olivia! You have always been right!" Replied Vega. *"When? When can you be at my home?"* Asked Vega.

"I'm not sure – but I'll be there as soon as I possibly can! I still remember where you live – so, as soon as I get there I will let you know?" I said, as I attempted to recall the map in my mind that I had made which I knew would lead me back to Vega's home. I was always good at finding my way back to somewhere that I had already been to before.

"Ok then, Melissa – I will see you soon!" Said Vega – before he hung up the phone. And I knew that the next time that I heard his voice I would be looking into his eyes – which I had to admit did make me smile.

Chapter Nineteen:
"Vis-à-vis"

When I arrived at the main gate of Vega's home, to my surprise the large automatic metal gates were already wide open and allowing anyone who was anybody to enter and exit at their leisure – however, I did not immediately drive through the main gate, I pulled up just before and I parked the red Mercedes where it could not directly be seen by anyone observing the long driveway that led to the huge house.

I couldn't see any other vehicles but my own – so I did not know what, nor who, to expect was already there; however, it was already apparent that someone was there.

I stepped out of the Mercedes, and then I started to look around for Vega – after all this was the exact spot where he had told me to expect him when I spoke to him on the phone; however, he was nowhere to be seen. I did give a thought to calling him again – but, for some reason, something was telling me that I shouldn't.

It was mid-afternoon by now, and the sun was high in the sky – not the most optimum time of the day to expect a vampire to be walking around, I was guessing; but Vega did say to meet him where I was, and if Vega was anything at all he was a man of his word. So, I waited, for 20 minutes – which felt like 20 hours, quite frankly – and then I decided that I had waited long enough, and I started to walk through the main gate and up the long driveway a little, until I was within the grounds of Vega's house, and then I began to walk the perimeter to see if I could come across anything that might lead me to where Melissa was being held.

As I walked around the area surrounding Vega's home, I could definitely sense something in the air, I could definitely feel something in the ground, and I could definitely detect a vibration – like the after-shocks of an explosion of some sort? I do not remember feeling anything similar to this the last time that I was here at Vega's home – however, I didn't leave his house the entire time that I was there?

There was definitely something eerie about being there again? Within touching distance of Vega's house? Mostly because I was seemingly the only one there – even though I knew that I wasn't, and also because… because there was no other sound to be heard but the beating of my own heart in my chest.

Then – as I continued to walk in an anti-clockwise direction around the grounds of Vega's home – I decided to reach out in my mind and try to communicate with Melissa telepathically, if she was in fact able to respond?

"Melissa, this is Mum – I'm here! I'm here! And I know that you are here, and I know that you are alive! Let me know that you are ok? Tell me… tell me where you are, and I will find you? Call out? Please? Wherever you are… wherever they have you – fight back! And let the blood-suckers know what happens when they mess with my daughter!" I said, as I spoke within my mind – hoping that my internal voice might carry far and wide to wherever Melissa was… it had before, so I hoped that it might again.

Then, I heard something – a faint sound at first; but the same one that continued to repeat and grow louder the more that I walked and the closer that I got to the interior of the grassy grounds of Vega's home: the unmistakable sound of a howl, and the call of a wolf – and I knew immediately, as did the Wolf, whose howl it was.

I began to run towards where I believed the howl was coming from, because I knew that it had to be Melissa – and then, in the distance, I saw them… I saw her… I saw Melissa, as the Wolf.

Immediately after she saw me, Melissa began to run towards me at full-speed – and the closer that the Wolf who was my daughter got to me, the more that I recognized and I realized that this Wolf had only one thing on their mind – and it wasn't a catch-up on where she had been and what she had been doing for the entire time since we last saw one-another? No, this Wolf meant to kill me – I could see it! I could feel it! I knew it! Which left with a dilemma: *What do I do? Do I change into the Wolf? And, if I do, then what is going to happen? Was I going to have to fight my own daughter? Potentially to the death? After I had been searching for her for so long?* But I knew that if I had any chance of getting

Melissa back at all, then I could only do that as the Wolf. So it was that reasoning that precipitated my opening the door for the Wolf to come out of me and transform my body into theirs. And then, I did what Melissa was doing: I ran towards my daughter, as the Wolf, and headlong into a confrontation.

I knew that it was probably the wrong time to be thinking about such a thing – however, I could not stop thinking about the last time that Melissa and I had seen one-another, and the last time that she was racing towards me in that black Mercedes – what seemed like a million years ago, by then. Isn't it funny what the mind brings to the surface at moments of extreme anxiety? And that moment that we felt one-another physically, after so long, felt just as painful as being hit head-on by a fast-moving car, for so many reasons.

I never thought that I would ever see the day when Melissa and I would be fighting each other – but that is exactly what happened.

As Melissa snapped at me with her teeth, in my mind I tried to reach out to her:

"Melissa, stop! What are you doing? It's me! It's Mum! Why are you doing this?" I asked her in my mind – hoping that she could somehow hear me; however, she did not reply.

As Melissa and I dangerously danced around one-another, it quickly became apparent to me that she was not the one in control – and perhaps neither was the Wolf? It was obvious to me that the Wolf in front of me was Melissa – but there was something in the way that she moved, in the way that she growled, in the way that showed her teeth, and there was something in their eyes, that told me: this was my daughter, but this was not my daughter – in other words: she was under the control of something, or someone else?

But what was controlling her? Or who? I asked myself.

"Melissa? Missy? Please! I don't want to hurt you!" I pleaded with Melissa in my mind.

However, the Wolf in front of me did not seem to share the same sentiment – and their attacks with their teeth got closer and closer to actually making an impact on me and causing me harm. But, this Wolf – Melissa – was a juvenile, and though they were definitely a fighter they were incredibly scrappy, and their

130

movements lacked any kind of precision – and that was how I was able to best them.

This Wolf – Melissa – was fast, and they were aggressive; however, they had not yet learned the art of anticipation, and they could not foresee what I was going to do next.

During our fight, while Melissa – as the Wolf – focused more on trying to catch me with their teeth… I, on the other hand, tried to tire Melissa out by moving out of her reach and not giving her any kind of opportunity to sink her teeth into me. We continued this constant dance for maybe 10 minutes, at the most – before I went on the offensive and I started to hit Melissa hard with the side of my head in an attempt to throw her off-balance, and it worked! And, over and over again, I would throw myself at Melissa with the full-force of my Wolf body, and then she would fall to the ground. And when I could see that she was becoming more and more fatigued, I again attempted to reach out to Melissa within my mind:

"Missy? Missy? Listen to me! This is not you! You have control! You can stop this! Melissa, head for the light! I know that right now you are alone in a seemingly dark space, surrounded by stars – but, as you look around yourself you will see a star that is brighter than all the others! And that star… that light is your way out! That star is your way back home! I know you are scared, and I know that you feel like that you cannot move or speak – but, believe me, you can take control! You can return to the light! You can be who you want to be! So, I am begging you, baby: fight! Fight! But, don't fight me – fight them! Fight the Wolf! Fight whichever blood-sucker is controlling you! Fight for your life! And come home to me! I love you, Melissa!" I said within my mind, as I stared into the eyes of the Wolf/Melissa – as I hoped with all my heart that Melissa could hear me and that she could do what I told her she had to do.

What I had told Melissa to do was what had taken me years to learn and to understand: that control went both ways, and if you wanted to take control of your destiny you might have to fight with yourself – and ultimately you will have to develop a relationship with the other half of your soul that is mutually beneficial for both sides? Though that relationship could take years to perfect, if at all?

I had no idea whether I had got through to Melissa – until I began to see a change in the way that the Wolf in front of me was moving… and that was when I realized that there appeared to be some kind of internal-turmoil rising within them: they seemed to be less aggressive towards me, their movements were slower, and the way that they looked at me seemed to be more… more acquiescent, if I were to describe the look that they had in their eyes?

And then, I tried again to reach Melissa:

"That's it! That's it, baby! Head towards the light! Fight it! Fight it! Scream! Shout! Take over! You can do it! You can do it!" I said within my mind.

After I finished saying all that I said, that was when the Wolf in front of me began to shake violently: their legs began to falter, and their eyes began to change – as did their entire body. And the Wolf's change continued until there was nothing left of the Wolf any longer – and there, on the ground, lay my daughter, Melissa, as human in form as she had been since the day she was born.

I immediately triggered my own transformation back into my human-form – and then I ran over to Melissa and I wrapped my arms around her. She was alive, and she was breathing – but she was in and out of consciousness, and in no fit state to talk coherently or move with any kind of independent coordination.

My instincts instantly kicked in and I quickly lifted Melissa off of the ground – both of us as naked as could be – and then I assisted her, walking as swiftly as we possibly could, back towards the main gate where the red Mercedes was parked. It took us a while to finally reach the car, as you can imagine – however, as we were making our way back, I retrieved the clothes that I had discarded before I changed into the Wolf and I used them to cover Melissa and keep her warm.

When we finally reached the car I helped Melissa into the passenger seat, and then I started the engine of the car and immediately turned on the heat of the car's A/C. Then I ran around to the other side of the car, I opened the drivers-side door, and then

I stepped in and sat in the drivers-seat – and I was fully ready to put the car into gear and drive as fast and as far away as possible. Until… until I started to think about Vega, and I began asking myself:

Where was he? He said that he would be waiting right here? But, where is he?

And then it occurred to me that they – the rebel vampires – must have captured Vega and they were probably holding him captive in his own house, and most likely torturing him at that very moment?

Which left me with another dilemma: Do I drive away with Melissa and forget all about Vega? Forget all about all that he had done for me, and try to forget what… what he meant to me? Or, do I leave Melissa alone again? While I… while I try to go and save Vega somehow? I was torn – both physically and psychologically, and also spiritually in a sense: because… because I knew that Vega did love me, and I… and I did… I do love him. And it was the love that I felt for both Vega and Melissa – individually and differently – which made me do what I did next: I left my phone, I left the keys to the car, and then I made the heart-wrenching decision to leave Melissa alone in the car, and I ran as fast as I could in the direction of Vega's house – changing into the Wolf, as I picked up speed, and as I ran faster and faster.

When I reached the front of the house, the normally automatically opening front-doors were wide open – as if they had been broken off of their hinges – and there were numerous black Mercedes cars and vans parked in the driveway. However, I did not hesitate, nor slow down to see if anybody was actually in the vehicles or not – I raced right on through the front-entrance of Vega's mansion, and I used my senses and my instincts to guide me to where Vega was. I didn't see anybody, at first – but after a few minutes I started to hear voices echoing all around the house: one of which I recognized as belonging to Vanguard:

"This is how it ends, your majesty!" I heard Vanguard say.

I followed Vanguard's voice to a large room, on the ground floor of the west-wing of the house, which appeared at first glance to be a gallery of artwork with paintings and sculptures on its walls

– however, at that moment in time, this room was more than a gallery: it was… something else.

When I looked around the corner of the room's entrance, and into the room, I saw… I saw Vega tied to a large wooden post, facing the large glass window that faced the front-garden of the mansion's estate, and he… Vega appeared to be in excruciating pain.

"How long have you wished for this? Hmm? How many nights was this not your dream? Well, this is it! And I consider it a privilege to be the one to deliver you to this moment!" Said Vanguard, as he walked around the post that Vega was tied up to with his hands behind his back.

"And to think, I actually believed that you were already dead? How? How could I have ever believed that you could be killed by such an ineffective malcontent as this vampire?" Said Vanguard, as he pointed to Vincent – who was being restrained by several male vampires behind the post that Vega was tied to. Val was also there – but she was looking away from Vincent, and instead she followed Vanguard's every move with her eyes.

"You see, he assured me that you were dead? He swore on his life that he had slain you? And yet, here you are! Here! You! Are! I… I suppose the only person who I can blame is myself? How could I have ever expected someone to kill you? Someone who did not know you as well as I do? I mean, we have known each other for… what? 200 years? Give or take a decade? Right? And that is why I realize now, in retrospect, that I should have been the one to kill you when the time came. I was… I was your most loyal confidant. I was… I was your friend! I was… I was your son! I was the one who you entrusted all your secrets and plans to! I… I was the one who you discussed the potential story-lines of your books with – and I like to believe that, perhaps, I was your muse?

However… however, then *she* came on the scene! *Her!* And that was when I began to see a change in you that I did not like: weakness… love – and what makes it worse now is the knowledge that you fell in love with… with a mangy werewolf? I mean, how could you? Your majesty, how could you allow yourself to do such a thing? You were our king? Our god?

But when I look at you now, I no longer see the king... the god who I used to know when I first met you. All I see is... all I see is someone who holds no other value to me than that of a human! And, when I take your life, I will not mourn you! I will not shed a tear! I will not allow you to be remembered! And... and I will make sure to discontinue every one of your books from publication, and then burn every one that I can find on a huge bonfire that will be seen for miles around!

And then... and then I will find little Miss *Olivia Hunter* – if there is indeed anything left of her once her daughter has taken more than a few bites of flesh and fur out of her? And I will make sure that she too will simply disappear. And then, I will be even more proactive in bringing the age of humanity to an end – so that the age of Vampire superiority can begin in earnest!" Said Vanguard, as his voice echoed in every direction – from floor to ceiling.

I knew that I could not just sit around and do nothing to help Vega – and that was why I readied myself to leap upon Vanguard and kill him at the earliest opportunity, before he could succeed in killing Vega.

However, before I could make any kind of a move, Vanguard raced over to where Vincent was being restrained – and he immediately grabbed a hold of Vincent's neck with his fangs and he ripped it open, and a torrent of blood instantly began to gush out of him and all over the floor, instantly bringing Vincent to his knees and into a pool of his own blood.

Vanguard then turned back around – his lips and his chin still covered in Vincent's blood – and he looked towards the wooden post that Vega was tied to with a look in his eyes that looked like a combination of pleasure and rage.

Vega said nothing, Vega did nothing – however, Val and the other vampires looked at both Vincent's now dead body and Vanguard's smiling face with expressions of shock on their faces – especially Val, who looked at Vincent with a tangible expression of sadness and loss on an unimaginable scale.

I recognized the expression on Val's face, because I still recalled wearing the same one on multiple occasions when I used to get out of bed and I looked in the mirror at my own reflection, after I lost… after I lost Terry. So, I knew exactly what she was feeling – and I believed I knew exactly why she was feeling the way that she was: she had just lost somebody who she loved.

"You see… you see, I am also a man of my words! And let Vincent's death here be a reminder to all that I do not excuse missed opportunities, nor failure! I am now the king! And when Vega here is no more than ash, I will do, and I will make real, what was once only a dream of his: a world solely of Vampires! Where and when we will only keep a group of humans to feed upon at our leisure, perhaps?" Said the psychopathic and sycophantic Vanguard, as he walked around the large room – before he finally stopped between where Vega was tied up, and where Val was also standing and looking up at Vega with tears in her eyes.

"And you, *Valkyrie* – you will be my queen! For the first time in our history there will be both a king and a queen who will rule over all others!" Said Vanguard, as he put his right-hand against the left-cheek of Val's face – and then he proceeded to rub her face with his thumb.

Vanguard was such a sleazy, blood-sucking, murderous, scumbag! And I just wish that I had been the one to kill him – however, Val beat me to it when she quickly knocked Vanguard's right-hand away from her face and she then sank her teeth into his neck… and she did to him what he had only moments ago done to Vincent.

Vanguard immediately put his right-hand up to his throat in a failed attempt to try and stop the blood that was pouring from his neck – and he even tried to plead with his attacker:

"Why? Why?" Said Vanguard, as he struggled to speak – as his own blood covered his fingers, as well as the black-suit that he was wearing.

"You… you… trait-tor! You… you… I… I… I am… I am… your… king!" Vanguard sputtered, as he stared wide-eyed at Val – who looked relatively content in comparison.

"YOU… ARE… NOT… MY… KING!" Screamed Val.
"You are a psychopath! You are the harbinger of death! You murdered the man I loved! And… and you had to be stopped!

I can't believe that I was stupid enough to follow you for as long as I did? And I can't believe that I was stupid enough to ever believe anything that you said? But, I won't make the same mistake twice!" Said Val – before she pulled Vanguard's hand away from his neck and she bit into him again and again, until he was on his knees and dying in what must have been excruciating pain.

And all throughout everything that happened, Vega just... he remained relatively stoic, as he continued to look out the window – however, with what looked like a tear on the verge of falling from his right-eye, as if he was sad about everything that had played out: including the death of Vanguard?

I just stood there. Stunned. And even if I could talk, or make any kind of understandable sound, I don't know if I would have been able to – but what could I have possibly said? Sometimes words are not enough to describe the simply indescribable.

Then, Val walked over to where Vega was and with the assistance of the other remaining vampires in the room helped to lower Vega to the floor and untie the binds that held him – which I am sure he could have easily broke free of if he had wanted to?

Chapter Twenty:
"A Vendetta of Vampires"

V ega stood up, he looked Val straight in the eye, and then he said:
"Thank you, Val! I know how difficult that must have been for you to see, and to do? And to all of you, I implore you to listen to what I have to say and think long and hard about what your response will be? I know that Vanguard must have told you many things, and I know that he must have made you believe many things? About me? About us? About the world? About his interpretation of our existence? And some of the things that he may have told you might even have had a ring of truth to them? But, I can guarantee to you that the majority of the things that he told you were lies, fabrication, and fantasy – in order for him to disguise his true motives for power and dominance!"

"I knew him! I knew Vanguard for centuries, and he was loyal! However, in all the time that I knew him, I saw within him the same self-destructive tendencies and beliefs that led him to do what he has done. There were times when I had to temper his extreme thoughts and feelings, for fear that he would not only harm himself, but others also?" Said Vega, as he looked into the eyes of every vampire standing within the spacious room – before he quickly took a hold of both of the curtains that hung either-side of the towering window, and he pulled them together, just before an extremely bright burst of sunlight came streaming in.

Val looked into the eyes of all the other vampires in the room, beginning with Vega, and then she let her feelings be known to all who could hear her.

"He... He might have been a murderer – but he was not completely crazy? He... He might have believed some very outlandish things, and he may have been planning to do some things that might have seemed revolutionary and self-destructive? But, he had a vision for a better life and a better world for us all? And something else that I want to make crystal-clear, is the fact that what I did I didn't do for you, your majesty! And though I may have saved you – thanks mostly to what you communicated to me telepathically – I am afraid to say that I do not know if I can be to you who I used to be? I have been irrevocably changed by what I have seen, and by what I have felt. And though I may call you *your majesty* – I no longer seek your blessings, nor your leadership? I will no longer worship you as I once did either? I... I... I just lost somebody... someone who I loved – and I don't mean Vanguard, I mean..."

"I know, Val!" Replied Vega immediately – and then he took a step back and he addressed everybody at once:

"The recent events have been trying for us all – and it is possible that none of us will ever be the same, because of what we have experienced? However, everything happens for a reason – nothing is ever accidental, nor coincidental. Every one of us lives a life full of purpose, and every one of us have a drive within us that at times can feel overwhelming? And that is why I understand why you would choose to take a step away from me, especially – but remember, no matter how far you go, you will always be a vampire!" Said Vega.

"Your majesty, we do not need you to remind us of who we are! Quite frankly, you are lucky that I did not feed upon you when I was staring down at your lifeless body in your girlfriend's home before we burned it to the ground?" Said Val with an amused expression on her face.

"I know, Val! I know! And for that I am extremely grateful!" Replied Vega with a smirk.

"In fact, you have Vincent to thank for that, your majesty – since he was the one who stopped me from ravaging you?" Said Val, as a tear fell down her left-cheek.

"That I also know, Val! And, in turn, I forgive Vincent for his actions and I absolve him of his crimes against me! As do I forgive all of you in this room! And I am sorry that he died because of me... because he did not kill me – even though he truly believed that he had?" Said Vega, as he looked into Val's eyes – and then he took a quick side-glance to where I was standing and he smiled.

139

"Even though you no longer wish to receive my blessings, I nonetheless offer you my hope that you will find that which you are searching for. As do I offer my blessings to all of you, because each and every one of you, individually, also have a choice to make: to leave my home and to say nothing of what has taken place here, nor speak of what Vanguard had planned to do? Or, you all stay and you pledge your allegiance to me – and in turn I will reward you all handsomely? However, if any one of you do ever seek to challenge me, or plot to overthrow me again – let's just say that you will suffer the consequences! I will give you all time to consider your positions – but, in the meantime, I ask you to assist me by cleaning up your own mess, and get rid of Vanguard's body? Vincent's body, on the other hand, I leave to you, Val, to take care of as you mourn his passing?" Said Vega, as he looked into the eyes of the vampires.

"Thank you, your majesty!" Said Val, as she stared at Vega and gave him a slight bow of the head – before she too took a side-glance in my direction with a look in her eyes that I could tell was not one of overflowing adoration… more like a look of daggers, to be honest?

I did not wish to stand in the doorway any longer – especially not now, as it was made quite clear to me that I was not welcome – so I decided to turn-tail and leave Vega's house.

However, just as I was about to walk out of Vega's mansion, I felt the gentle sensation of someone stroking the fur on my back – which made me immediately stop and turn around to see who was behind me: and, of course, it was Vega.

"Leaving so soon?" Asked Vega with a wide smile; "You don't want to stay for the feast?" He said, as he crouched down and looked into my eyes.

"I'm sorry that you and your daughter got dragged into this Vendetta of Vampires – and though I know this is not the right time for us to discuss what happens next, I… I would like to see again soon, if you don't mind? And, please, feel free to continue to use both the apartment in Birmingham as your home and the Mercedes as your form of transport? And, of course, please offer my sincerest apologies to your daughter for all that she has been through?" Said Vega with what looked like a smile of genuine compassion.

"But, for the time being, I would like to invite you both to stay here for as long as you wish? There are still some of the clothes that were bought for you upstairs in one of the spare-rooms that you can use to change into?" Said Vega – who I knew was only trying to be considerate; however, in all honesty, I was still more than a little upset with him… and I was also more than a little unsettled at the prospect of spending even more time here with these vampires, especially after what I had just witnessed.

However, I knew that I had to think about the well-being of both Melissa and I – and I too felt guilty about what my daughter had been subjected to by these rebel vampires. So, that was why – with Melissa in mind – I asked Vega for a favor, within my mind:

"Let me change back into my human-form? Let me change into some fresh clothes? Allow us to stay the night here, so that Melissa can rest and recuperate a little? And then, in the morning, she and I will leave? Is… would that be ok with you?" I asked nervously within my mind, as I looked into Vega's sparkling eyes.

"Of course, Olivia! Of course!" Replied Vega with a smile.

"Ok, well… Just let me go upstairs and change – and then I will race down to the bottom of the driveway, and I will… I will…"

"Why don't I go and get Melissa? And then drive her up here in the Mercedes – while you freshen-up?" Said Vega with a smile.

"I… I…" I said hesitantly – secretly questioning in the back of my mind whether Vega's motives were genuine, or perhaps nefarious. However, I only considered the possibility that he sought to harm Melissa in some way for an instant – until I replied: *"Sure! Sure – I guess, that… that would be ok!"*

And then Vega put both of his hands around my face, and he said calmly:

"Have no fear, Olivia! I promise you I will not run off with your daughter – nor do anything nefarious or untoward to her!" He said, as he attempted to settle my concerns by repeating my own inner thoughts back to me – however, I could see in his eyes that he was feeling more than a little hurt at my insinuation of any ulterior motives that he may have… but he made no verbal comment of his disappointment.

"Thank you! Thank you, Vega! I… I… I will be upstairs if anybody needs me? And, please, let me know when Melissa gets here? She… she is in no fit state to know what is happening, nor is she wearing any clothes? So, I would appreciate it if… if you allow me to attend to her alone?" I asked.

"Of course, Olivia!" Replied Vega, as he nodded his head up and down in agreement. "I will personally inform you when the red Mercedes is again parked in the front-driveway. And when I return, I will arrange for some food to be prepared for you both – as well as a bedroom for you to share during your stay here. Let me know if you require anything else while you are here? But, for now, I am sure that who and what you want the most right now is your daughter – so I will waste no more time, and I will retrieve her at once!" Said Vega with a smile – before he turned around and walked out of the house, and then he went to get Melissa and bring her back to me.

Chapter Twenty-One:
"I love you"

That night, as Melissa and I were lying in bed facing one-another – Melissa with her eyes closed, flickering, and no doubt dreaming about god knew what, as she slept seemingly peacefully... while I just lay there, with my eyes open as wide as could be, as I looked at my beautiful daughter. I still recalled doing what Melissa and I were doing then when she was still a baby – which, to me, still felt like yesterday.

I lost so much time. I missed watching Melissa grow up from a newborn baby to a beautiful little girl – ten long years, in fact – and I promised myself, and Melissa, that I would never again allow us to be kept apart. And look what happened? I almost lost her for good – and all because of me? Because I fell in love with a vampire? And because that same vampire fell in love with me – and because the other vampires didn't like the idea of this, they decided to draw me and my daughter into their vendetta? However, after some time away from each other, beyond both of our control – here we are again: mother and daughter.

I love my daughter – and I just hope that she won't suffer any ill-effects as a result of the traumatic events that she has no doubt been subjected to? I can't wait until she wakes up, so that we can talk about everything that has happened and build bridges between one-another – and come to understand what has happened to both of us? But, for right now, I am just so glad to have her back – and no small reason for that must be placed at the feet of Vega, because I think he knew exactly what he was doing? And, I believe that, though he may be a vampire, his heart is in the right place when it comes to his people, and to me?

Vega loves me – that which I know for certain. And I actually believe that he would do almost anything for me?

I wish I could climb inside Melissa's head and see what she is dreaming of, and know what she is thinking and feeling. But, I guess that I ultimately might have to accept the fact that I may never know all that she has been through? Now I know what my parents would have experienced had they known exactly what I was and what I went thought when I was Melissa's age. But, the most important thing is that she is safe! And if I have anything to say about it, she is not going anywhere without me ever again!

I tried to sleep, I honestly did – but something... someone continued to keep me wide-awake.

As I looked at Melissa, sleeping soundly next to me, I envied her in that moment – because, even after all that she had been through, she could sleep. Of course, Melissa had not yet fully regained consciousness since Vega brought her back to the house – but I could not stop thinking that I would give anything to be able to sleep also? But I couldn't sleep, because I had Vega on my mind.

I suppose it was the thought that at that moment he and I were in the same house – but it was the first time since we became intimate with one-another that we had not shared the same bed while within close proximity to each other?

There was only one way that I knew how I was going to get over this extreme bought of insomnia – and that was to get out of bed, and go and see the one who was keeping me awake. So, I did just that, as quietly as I could so as to not disturb Melissa.

I got out of bed. I walked barefoot out of the bedroom that Melissa and I were sharing – literally tip-toing over the dark-wooden floorboards – wearing only a white vest and a pair of black and white poker-dotted shorts, and then I made my way down the long red hallway to Vega's bedroom.

When I entered Vega's bedroom, I immediately saw him standing next to the large window, seemingly looking up at the stars, wearing only his red robe, with both hands behind his back. He didn't appear to know I was there – but I knew that he did really, and he was just trying to be all mysterious. I almost didn't want to disturb him – however, I couldn't help myself.

"Am I disturbing you?" I asked quietly, as I stood next to him.

"Of course not, Olivia! Please, share my view of the stars with me?" Said Vega calmly – however, without even moving an inch to look at me, and instead he continued to gaze up at the stars.

"I... I... I couldn't sleep. I... I... I don't know what is wrong with me? But I... I..." I said nervously, as I too looked up at the clear night-sky that presented us with a spectacular skyscape of twinkling lights.

"Beautiful! Isn't it?" Remarked Vega.

"Yes, it is! Very beautiful! You must never get bored of looking at this view?" I asked, as I began to feel this overwhelming wave of emotion begin to rise within me.

"Yes, very beautiful! But, do you know what? And this might sound as cheesy as hell, but I am still going to say it – no matter how beautiful and breathtaking the night-sky may be, it, nor anything or anybody, could ever compare to the exquisiteness that is your perfect and beautiful face, Olivia! I... I have been intoxicated by your breathtaking smile since I first laid my eyes upon you – not to mention your truly hypnotizing eyes? You... you are... you are the most beautiful and gorgeous woman in the entire universe!" Said Vega, still continuing to look out the window – while I was a complete storm of hormones as I stood next to him, completely and utterly intoxicated by him... just as I had been since the moment that I first laid my eyes upon him.

"You... you don't know how hard this is? I... I have never felt like this before for anyone? I... I love you!" I said, as the rising wave of emotions within me overflowed and tears started to fall from my eyes.

"I... I know you do, Olivia! However, after tonight, I believe that you and I may not each other for a while?" Said Vega.

I immediately turned my head to look at him.

"Why?" I asked tearfully.

"I... I just got word from America. It... it seems that Vanguard's insurrection may be on the verge of spreading across the pond and infecting our American cousins? The population of vampires in the U.S. is considerable – however, it would not take much for word to spread and a fresh rebellion to form there, especially if they over there were to hear more about what has been taking place here in the U.K? So, I must travel to the U.S. as soon as possible in order to quash any sign of rebellion before the spark becomes a raging fire!" Said Vega – noticeably, and uncharacteristically, emotional.

"But? But, what happened? Did someone who was here talk? Was it… was it Val?" I asked, as I stared at Vega – unable to stop my tears from falling one after the other.

"I… I don't know, Olivia? All that I know is that word has already spread – and that if I want to maintain my position and my authority, I… I will have to show the rest of the vampires of this world that I am still their king and that I do not tolerate any kind of challenge to my leadership! The very equilibrium of vampire society could be at stake should I fail?" Explained Vega.

"But? But, how long will you be gone?" I asked.

"I… I don't know, Olivia! Days? Weeks? Months?" Replied Vega, as he closed his eyes – as if he were trying to stop himself from crying.

"But, I love you! I love you, Vega!" I said through a veil of tears.

"I know you do, Olivia! And, I love you!" Said Vega, as he opened his eyes again – and then he turned to his right to look me in the eye, and he said: "Don't cry, Olivia! This… this is as hard for me as it is for you!" He said, as he reached out his arms and he pulled me close to him.

I was inconsolable.

As Vega held me, and as I held him as tightly as I could – we both did not want to let go of each other for anything.

"I'm sorry!" I said, as I rested my head upon his chest – as I listened to his heart beating and racing away with itself.

"For what?" Asked Vega, as he kissed the top of my head.

"For not believing you?" I replied regretfully.

"It's ok, Olivia! If I were you I wouldn't believe myself either – but one thing I need you to believe, and never to forget, is that I love you and I always will! And though I must leave you soon – you will never leave my heart, nor my thoughts! And I promise you that we will see each other again! I swear! Ok?" Said Vega – before I let go of him, I looked into his sparkling eyes, and then I lifted up my head and I kissed him on the lips.

We stayed in each other's embrace for what seemed like hours – until we finally pulled away from one-another, and then we… and then Vega guided me over to his bed, where we made love to each other all night long… until I finally fell to sleep in his arms.

●

The next morning – to my utter surprise, quite frankly – I awoke to find Vega still lying next to me and still seemingly sleeping soundly. I was surprised, because I did not expect him to still be there when I woke up. And, as I watched him sleeping next to me, I knew that I could not say goodbye to him – but I also knew that when he woke up he would no doubt immediately be traveling to the United States? But, like I said, I knew that I could not say goodbye to him – which left with a dilemma, as well as some questions to ask myself that only I could answer:

What am I going to do? Should I go with him to America? Should I stay with him no matter what? Should I help him however I can? But, what about Melissa? She just came back? And do I really want to expose her, and myself, to a wider world of vampires? And potentially put ourselves in even deeper danger than we have already been in? But, I love Vega? And I don't want to let him go?

However, every time I thought about Vega and I being together, I was always brought back to asking the same question:

What was best for Melissa?

And I knew in my heart that this life – life with Vega – was not the best life for Melissa, and she deserved something more.

So, it was as I took one last long look at Vega – as he lay silently next to me – that I decided that things had to change, and I… I had to leave… I had to leave his bed… I had to leave his life… and Melissa and I needed to leave his house and go home.

I left Vega's bed in tears – but I also knew that I could not leave before I looked at his handsome face one last time, and I gave him one last gentle kiss on his lips... which I did to the sound of my

147

heart breaking in my chest. And then I quietly walked out of Vega's bedroom, and I made my way back down the red hallway to the bedroom where Melissa had been sleeping all night long – and just as she was beginning to wake up.

"Hey, baby!" I whispered, as I walked towards Melissa – as she opened her eyes wide, and then immediately jumped up onto the bed, reached out her arms, and then gave me the most amazing hug I had ever been given.

I felt uncontrollably overwhelmed with a maelstrom of emotions as I hugged Melissa – so much so that I immediately began to break down in tears again.

"Mum! Mum! I... I missed you so much! I... I... I was beginning to think that I would never see you again?" Said Melissa, as she too began to cry – as she held me as tightly as she could.

"I know, baby! I know! I've missed you so much too! I... I never stopped looking for you, and I thought about you every second of every day!" I said, as I sat down on the bed next to her.

"I know, Mum! I... I... I tried to fight! I tried to run! I tried to escape – but they... they did things... they made me do things! I... I... I couldn't... I couldn't control... I couldn't stop it! I couldn't break-free! And then, I heard your voice in my mind – and I knew what I had to do... and I knew that I had to get back to you! I... I'm sorry! I'm so sorry! I... I... I'm sorry that I never told you about what was happening to me! I'm sorry that I didn't tell you that they forced me to go with them! But they said that if I didn't go with them that they would kill you! I... I... I was just trying to keep you safe!" Said Melissa, as she struggled to get her words out – as she was no doubt reliving in her mind every torturous moment of the last few months.

I still could not believe that I did not see what she was going through – but, in my defense, I guess that I was more than a little distracted at the time and blinded by the haze of our new life, and of course by Vega.

"Missy, it's ok! You have nothing to be sorry about! I'm the one who should be sorry? And I am sorry that all this happened –

and that you got wrapped up in all of this!" I said, as I let go of Melissa and I looked into her tear-filled eyes.

"But now is not the time to wallow in our pain and sadness – because you and I need to leave this place, and right now!" I said, as got up from the bed and I immediately began collecting together all of our belongings and then throwing them into a small hold-all bag.

"Where are we going? And... and where are we now? Whose house is this?" Asked Melissa, as she followed me rushing around the room with her eyes – as I simultaneously packed a bag, as well as got dressed into some clothes.

"It's a... it's a long story, baby! And I promise that I will tell you everything that has happened! But, for right now, we need to get out of here!" I said – as Melissa stepped out of the bed and she began to get dressed into the clothes that I had set down on the bed besides her.

"But? But?" Said Melissa – noticeably and naturally confused about what was going on – as she began to get dressed also.

"I know that you don't know what is going on, nor where we are – but if we don't leave this place right now, then we are never going to leave!" I said.

As soon as we were both fully dressed, and as quickly as we could, Melissa and I left the bedroom that we had shared for the night, we raced down the red hallway to the grand staircase that stretched from the ground floor all the way up to the fourth floor of this epic mansion that was Vega's home – and then we ran out through the somewhat newly repaired front-door to the red Mercedes that was parked in the driveway.

"Oh my god, Mum! Is this ours?" Asked Melissa, as soon as she saw and as soon as she realized that the red Mercedes that we were running towards was going to be our transport away from where we were to where we were going.

"Whose car is this?" Asked Melissa, as she took a step back and looked at the Mercedes as if she was in awe of it.

"It's ours – but don't get too attached to it!" I replied immediately, as I lifted up the driver's side door and I stepped into the drivers-seat – and Melissa did the same, on the passenger-side, after she finally realized that the Mercedes had doors that opened like Doc Brown's DeLorean from *Back to the Future.*

"This! This is awesome! This is... this is beautiful! This... this must have cost a lot?" Said Melissa, as she stepped inside the car and then pulled down the passenger-side door with a *clunk.*

"Where did you get this from? And where... where is our other car?" Asked Melissa.

"Don't worry, baby – I'll explain everything, just as soon as we get back home!" I said, as I started the engine of the Mercedes with aid of the ENGINE STOP/START BUTTON, and the car instantly roared to life.

"Did we win the lottery, or something?" Asked Melissa with a look of glee on her face.

"Not exactly!" I replied immediately, as I pushed down on the accelerator pedal and then began driving down the long driveway as fast as I could – before then exiting the grounds of the mansion's estate through the still wide-open gates.

Melissa's attention soon moved on from her fascination with the Mercedes to the subject of her stomach:

"Is there anything to eat at home? I'm starving! I could so go for a pizza right now?" Said Melissa – who had not eaten anything since I did not know when, because she had not been in any fit state to eat anything that the person who prepares Vega's food had prepared for us to eat. I, myself, had only eaten one half of a cheese sandwich – so I too was hungry.

"Don't worry – we'll get something at a service station on our way down there!" I replied.

"Down there?" Asked Melissa; "Down where? I thought we were going home?" She asked – however, looking very confused.

"We are! We... we are going home! But just not to the one we recently called *home*... because... because that one is no longer there!" I replied – however, being very coy about the details of where exactly we were going and what had happened to our former house.

I followed the road signs that directed us to the nearest Motorway junction, which we could use to get on to the nearest Motorway that headed south-west – looking in both side-mirrors of the car as we drove farther and farther away from Vega's mansion to see if we were being followed.

"Mum, I don't understand? Where are we going? Tell me?" Asked Melissa with a frown.

"Look, we… we… we're just going to stay with auntie Aiyana for a while! Until everything up here settles down!" I said, as I revealed to Melissa that we were going back to the south coast of England, back to where we came from, and back to where Aiyana lived – our amazing friend who had cared for Melissa for the first 10 years of her life, while I was away being the Wolf, and the woman who saved me by bringing me back to life.

"Does she know we're coming to stay with her?" Asked Melissa with a look of surprise on her face.

"No – but I can't see why she would have a problem with us just showing up unexpected, do you? I'm sure that she has missed us both and has been wondering how we are doing, and what has been going on? Just imagine how happy she will be when she sees us?" I said with a smile, as I continued to look straight ahead and as I continued to follow all the signs that directed me towards the motorway that we would need to take to get Melissa and me back home to the New Forest.

"Yeah, of course – but… but I still don't get why we can't just go back to the house?" Asked Melissa.

"And I'll tell you why later – but, just so you know, we are never going back to that house!" I replied with a feeling of frustration bubbling up inside of me, because I knew I was soon going to have to explain to Melissa that our house was destroyed by a fire – or, more accurately, by an act of terrorism.

"But, what about school? What about your job? What about my friends?" Asked Melissa, as she gave me a confused stare.

"We will talk about what happened… later, Missy! I promise! But, for right now, we need to go back home! You can send Aiyana a message, if you want? Let her know we're on our way? Or you can call her? My phone is in that bag back there, behind my seat?"

I replied – as I tried to swiftly change the subject away from what had happened while Melissa was away, for the time being.

"Fine! Ok! I'm sure that you will tell me everything when you're ready?" Said Melissa in a sardonic tone of voice.

"Why don't we listen to some music while we drive, huh?" I said, as I fiddled around with the many buttons and switches on the centre console of the car just below the windscreen – as I attempted to find a radio station that played some music that we could both listen to on our road-trip, which preferably played songs that I already knew, which had lyrics that I could clearly understand. I tuned in the radio to one of my favourite radio stations – just as Dolly Parton's classic *"I Will Always Love You"* began playing, whose version of the song I had always preferred to that of Whitney Houston's cover-version, I have to say.

And for the rest of our long journey back to the south-coast – though briefly pulling over mid-way to get some drive-through fast-food – that was what Melissa and I did: I drove, I listened to some songs on the radio, and I… I thought about who, and what, I was leaving behind: namely, Vega. And I was constantly having to stop myself from periodically bursting into tears again and again at the thought of just leaving Vega the way that I had.

While I was busy driving and thinking, Melissa used the phone that Vega had given me to inform Aiyana that we were on our way – as well as a means to go on the internet to catch-up on everything that was going on in the world that she had missed, and also to watch whatever "trending videos" were on YouTube that she had missed while she was disconnected from reality.

In no time at all, after a couple of hours of non-stop driving, we finally arrived back in the New Forest. Back to the old stomping grounds of Me, Melissa, and the Wolf as well – and we did not stop until we arrived at Aiyana's cottage. And when we finally arrived at the front-door of Aiyana's cottage we only had to wait for a few seconds, after we rang the doorbell, before Aiyana appeared with a smile on her face and with open arms for both Melissa and I.

Chapter Twenty-Two:
"The Letter"

O ver the next few hours, following our return home – our return to Aiyana's home, but also somewhere that Melissa considered home because she had spent her childhood growing up there – Melissa and I told Aiyana everything about what had happened since we moved to our new, now non-existent, home in the Centre of England. Everything from Melissa knowing that she was about to change into a Wolf for the first time, to our forced confrontation with one-another as a result of psychological conditioning by the rebellious wanna-be vampire king, Vanguard.

As for my side of the story, I tried to skim over the finer details of my relationship with Vega – and on that subject I knew that neither Aiyana, nor Melissa, wanted, nor needed, to know everything. However, listening to Melissa tell her story of what happened to her while she was being held prisoner by the vampires was absolutely heartbreaking for me to hear – and it no doubt must have been a thousand times worse for Melissa to relive? Because, unlike me, Melissa did not hold back at all in describing the abuse that she was subjected to.

In comparison to what we had been through, Aiyana told us that her life had been relatively quiet for the most part – the highlight of the past few months being when she was walking to the local Post Office and she found a £20 note lying on the floor, which she had not told a single soul about before us. Aiyana told us that she had mostly been focusing on her paintings – the sales of which she had received a modest income from, and the local gallery had been kind enough to both put her paintings on display for everybody to admire, as well as handle the sales of her paintings for her without taking any kind of commission for doing so. And Aiyana did seem happy. She seemed content. And she seemed to be living the life she always wanted, where she wanted, and she was able to do exactly what she wanted, when she wanted – in her words, her life as it was then was: *"A dream come true"*.

Melissa and I, on the other hand, were now homeless, jobless, penniless, and in desperate need of a purpose – beyond being the Wolf.

It was soon evening – and as Aiyana and Melissa continued to talk and catch up with one-another, I instead retreated to my old bedroom – and it was just as the moon could be seen just above the horizon that I sat down on my bed and I started to unpack a couple of things from the bags that Melissa and I had brought with us. And, as I took things out one by one, I slowly uncovered an envelope with my name on it – the same envelope that Vega had given to me after I left him to move into the apartment that he had arranged for me.

I had honestly forgotten all about that envelope, that letter – and now that I was holding it in my hands I found myself afraid to open it and read it, because I had no idea whatsoever what Vega had written to me. I almost put the letter back into the bag from where I found it – but… but, in the same breath, I was also curious about what he might have said, and… and this letter was something that Vega wanted to communicate to me personally – and it could have been the last thing that he said to me.

And that was my reasoning for initially laying the envelope down on the bed besides me for a good long while – before I finally bit the bullet, I took a breath, I opened the envelope, and I read the hand-written letter from Vega.

●

Dear Olivia,

I suspect that by whatever time and place you choose to read this letter, you may already be wondering when, and if, your life will ever, and could ever, be normal again? However, you already know that things have not been "normal" for you in a very long time. But the reason that you do not live an "ordinary life" – in comparison to a great many people in this world – is because you are by no means ordinary... you are extraordinary in every way! And it is the fact that you are so blessed with the gift to be able to change yourself into a wild and ethereal spirit that makes you so extraordinary. And it is your pure heart and your generous soul that makes you stand out from the crowd of everybody else on this planet.

I have lived in this world for a very long time – however, in all the time that I have walked this Earth, I have never met anybody quite like you, Olivia! I only wish that you and I had met each other a long time before we did. However, I still maintain the belief that you and I must have known each other in another life? In another place? At another time? Because I feel like I have known you all my life!

I will always believe that you and I were meant to meet, meant to fall in love with one-another, to be together, and to share an unbreakable connection with one-another – however, I fear that our paths may one day diverge again and I might have to accept that our union may only have been meant to be for a short time. And if there does in fact come a time when either of us must choose whether to stay together, or to live apart, I know that no matter where we are, or who we are with, our love for one-another will never die and will continue to burn until the end of time.

I do not wish for this letter to be so long that it could easily become the length of a chapter in one of my books – so I will soon cut this correspondence short, before my words accidentally run away with themselves. However, before I do that, I would like to tell you something... something that you already know, but that which I enjoy telling to over and over again. And that something is that I love you! I love you, Olivia Hunter! And I always will!

Life can never be accurately predicted in great detail – however, that being said, I know with all that I am that I love you! I have always been meant to love you! And I will always love you!

So now I say goodbye to you, Olivia – but, of course, this is not truly a goodbye in the conventional sense? It is more of a see you soon! And I know for a fact that we will see each other again very soon – but, until then, I hope that you will look after yourself... and that you will do what your instincts tell you to do, and what the wolf in you tells you to do – because, if I know anything about you, and about the wolf inside you, it is that no matter what you are faced with you will continue to endure and outlive the adversary that is death from taking you before your time.

I love you!

-V

I… I was shaking after I finished reading Vega's letter, and I put it down on the bed. I was also unsuccessful in trying to hold back the flood of tears that was already streaming down my cheeks.

I sat there on my bed feeling… feeling absolutely awful! I felt so guilty! I felt so selfish! And I knew that I would most likely always feel this way – because… because I knew that no matter what Vega's letter had said, there was no going back.

I knew it – and the Wolf in Me knew it too. Everything happens for a reason… the die cannot be uncast… and what is done is done. I… I… I knew that I had to think about Melissa first now – because she was all that I had.

I wanted to scream! I wanted to shout! I wanted to… I wanted to be with Vega – but I knew that we couldn't be together, because we were literally from different worlds. But, saying all that, I would never hesitate at the opportunity to see him again – even if it were only for a second, one day?

But that moment was not the time – and I did not know when the right time would be, and I didn't know… I didn't… I didn't know what I should be feeling. All I knew for sure was that I didn't know what was going to happen next – however, I decided while I was still figuring everything out, at least for the moment, I would do what Vega advised me to do: listen to my instincts. So, I did exactly what my instincts told me to do: I laid down on my bed, I closed my eyes, and I allowed a wave of sleep to envelope me and then carry me away to me dreams.

Chapter Twenty-Three:
"Who are you?"

A week after Melissa and I returned home, on a sunny Wednesday afternoon – just after the rain stopped falling, and a beautiful blue sky was revealed – the three of us – Aiyana, Melissa, and I – decided to leave the cottage and go for a walk through the nearby woods.

I had always loved going for walks since I was a child – as well all the other outdoor activities that are available, if you know where to look.

Of course, being half-Wolf – you could say – I loved being outdoors and surrounded by nature at every turn, because that was my natural habitat… that was where I thrived… that was where I knew… and that was where I, as the Wolf, could be myself. Which was why I always jumped at the chance to return to my roots and spend as much time outside and doing all manner of things while I had the opportunity.

The last few months had been an incredibly stressful time for both Melissa and me – and we both considered our return home to the New Forest as a way for us to reboot and rejuvenate ourselves in mind, body, and spirit.

Aiyana was delighted to have us back, I could tell – and she had made every effort since we had been back to be as attentive as ever to both of us. The idea of us all going for a walk was Aiyana's – and for that, and for so much more, I could not have thanked her enough… because going for a walk in the place that I loved, with my beautiful daughter and my good friend, was just what I needed.

The intoxicating smell of the rain-soaked forest floor was amazing! The aroma coming from the trees was heavenly! The sound of the gentle breeze moving through the trees sounded to me like a beautiful symphony! And the warm sunshine upon my face felt extraordinary – and I felt so glad and so lucky to be back where my story began for me.

It wasn't cold in the slightest – however, we had all planned for the worst and we were all wearing the biggest and the warmest coats that we could find. My big black coat was sufficient – but no way as warm, nor as protective from the elements, as the coat of fur that I wore when I was the Wolf.

We walked through the forest of trees for maybe an hour, or two, talking about the weather, discussing what we were going to have for dinner that night, and basically just admiring the beauty of nature that we saw all around us.

I hadn't heard from Vega since I had been back, nor had I tried to contact him – but I was sure that he was most likely mad at me for not saying goodbye to him before Melissa and I left without a word to anybody.

Two days after we got back home, I drove the red Mercedes that Vega had given to me – which Melissa and I had used to return home – to a public carpark 20 miles away from where Aiyana's cottage was located, and after I cleaned it from roof to floor – both on the inside and on the outside, to try and erase any evidence that Melissa or I had ever been anywhere near it – I left it where I parked it, still with the keys inside, and I walked away. Cleaning that car was like a scene out of crime movie in which a criminal attempts to cover his tracks after he had committed a murder, or some-such – and though neither Melissa, nor I, had committed any crime whatsoever, in the Mercedes at least – I thought it best to be as thorough as possible and remove any physical breadcrumbs that could be retraced to us. First rule in keeping a secret: always cover your tracks.

After we left the Mercedes, Melissa and I were again without a form of transport – however, Aiyana did say that we could use her 4x4 any time we wanted. I did plan to get us another car, at some point – not to mention clear up some of the mess that we left behind up north; however, for the moment, Melissa and I were content to just enjoy our time being back home and not worrying too much about what was going to happen next.

It must have been around 3 o'clock in the afternoon, while we were still walking, that we all started to feel the temperature begin to drop – and it was then that we made a unanimous decision to cut our walk short and make a slow return home to the cottage.

It was just as we were within half a mile of the cottage, when we heard some fellow walkers approaching us from up ahead. And within the blink of an eye there in front of us we saw a young man with short-brown hair, dressed all in black, and a young blond-haired woman, dressed in every shade of green, walking towards us and holding onto the blue leash of a large black and white colored male dog that looked like a huskie – a fellow wolf if ever I saw one.

"Hi there!" Said the man with short-brown hair, as he stood with both hands inside his coat pockets.

"Hi!" I replied immediately with a smile – however, while instantly feeling this sensation of having déjà vu for some reason... even though, as far as I was aware, I had never seen either this man or this woman before in my life. But, saying all that, there was definitely something familiar about this man and this encounter that I couldn't put my finger on.

"How are you all doing today?" Asked the young man.

"We're ... we're doing good, thank you!" Said Aiyana with a smile – who did not appear to be experiencing what I was experiencing at that moment in time; but, in all honesty, even I had no idea what I was experiencing. "How are you?" Asked Aiyana in a familiar tone of voice – which made me wonder whether Aiyana knew who these people were.

"Very well, thank you!" Replied the blond-haired young woman with an American accent that sounded like she was from the south of the United States of America.

"You're American?" Asked Melissa with surprise in her voice.

"I am indeed! Just visiting for a short time with my husband here, and old Willie of course!" Said the blond-haired woman with a smile – who I also could have sworn I had seen before somewhere.

"Is he a huskie?" Asked Melissa, as she reached out her right-hand to the couple's dog.

I couldn't explain why it was that these strangers seemed so familiar. It was... it was... it felt like we had honestly just walked into an episode of the T.V. show *The X-Files,* or *Supernatural* – because... because this encounter was just too weird for words.

"Uh-huh! And don't worry, he doesn't bite! He loves giving "sugars" though – if you know what I mean? That's mainly what he wants to do most of the time, in fact – just give some love! Don't you, Willie?" Said the blond-haired woman, as she bent down to ruffle the fur of her dog.

"Where in the states are you from? I lived in North Dakota for a while – which I am sure you can tell from my accent?" Said Aiyana with a smile.

"Georgia! Well – more Tennessee, really?" Replied the blond-haired American woman with striking blue eyes.

"I thought so!" Said Aiyana; "So, you both having a good morning?" Asked Aiyana with a warm smile.

"Oh, absolutely! I love days like this! And I love going for long walks in a place just like this!" Said the British-sounding man with short-born hair.

And that was the moment when I felt like I couldn't wait any longer, before I asked this couple who they were – because, now more than ever, I truly believed that I knew them both from somewhere.

"Pardon me for asking this, but... but who are you both?" I asked – in an admittedly forward tone of voice, which was purely accidental.

"Excuse me?" Replied the short-haired British young man.

"I... I know that this might sound crazy – but... but I could have sworn that I had seen your face before? Both of your faces, actually? Maybe even all three of your faces?" I said, as I looked at the man, the woman, and their dog individually – sounding as crazy as I implied I might already be sounding.

"I... I don't think so? I mean, it's possible – I guess? But, we're only here for a short-time?" Said the short-haired British young man with a smile – who sounded like he was from up north somewhere? Birmingham, maybe?

"May I ask you your names?" I asked, as I walked closer to the couple – desperate to uncover the mystery of their identities.

"Olivia?" Said Aiyana immediately, as she looked at me with a frown; "Why do you need to know who they are?"

"Yeah, Mum – that's kind of rude, don't you think?" Said Melissa, as she too looked at me with an expression of confusion on her face.

"No, it's ok! Like I said, we're only here for a couple of days. I'm, err... I'm Mark... Mark Hastings – and this is my wife, Melissa! And you already know Will, of course!" Said "Mark" with a smile – as my head felt like it was on the verge of a meltdown, because... because their names were... their names were "Mark" and "Melissa": which sounded a lot like *"Marcus"* and *"Melis"*, from that origin story that Vega had told me about on the phone that time? That story about his parents? Vega's parents: *Marcus and Melis*? Mark and Melissa? And, in my mind, there was no way that these two people having those two names was a coincidence.

"Mark and Melissa? Mark and Melissa?" I asked over and over again – as the world felt like it was spinning. "It... it is so great to meet you both! It really is!" I said with a smile, as I reached out my right-hand to shake both of their hands.

"The same to you... all of you!" Replied Mark. "Is, err... is everything ok?" Asked Mark with a look of concern.

"Fine! Great! Yes, we're just... we're just out for a family walk through the woods! I... I know these trees like I know the back of my hand! This... this is where I became... this is where I first..." I began to say – until my words went absolutely nowhere, as did my train of thought.

"Yeah, it's nice! Very nice!" Said Melissa – Mark's wife – with a smile.

"Anyway, I'm sure that you both have somewhere else to be – and we have taken up far too much of your time already? So?" Said Aiyana politely, as she tried to allow the couple to continue on their walk.

"Not at all! It was lovely to meet y'all! Have a great rest of your day!" Said Melissa – Mark's wife – with a smile, as she and

Mark appeared to be on the verge of continuing with their walk – however, until I asked:

"Who are you? And, how do I know you?"

"I don't know, err... *Olivia*? I have never met you before in my life!" Said Mark – looking more intrigued than confused by my questions, if I was correctly interpreting the look that he was giving me.

"Do you know who I am?" I asked – desperate for an answer to this riddle of recognition before me.

"I'm afraid not? I only know your name, because your friend? Family-member? Just said it?" Said Mark.

"My name is Olivia... Olivia Hunter – does that name mean anything to you?" I asked, as I looked Mark in the eye.

"I don't think so?" Replied Mark immediately, as he looked back at me. "Who? Who are you?" He asked, as he stared at me – and as I stared at him, as I attempted to communicate with him who I was through telepathy.

"I... I... I'm not sure... that I... understand. You... you are... you are a... a..." Said Mark – before he slowly stepped away from me, and then he immediately rubbed his eyes.

"Hey! What are you doing?" Asked Melissa – Mark's wife – as she walked over to her husband, while simultaneously giving me a look of warning to back off.

"I'm... I'm sorry! I'm sorry! It's just that I think I know you both from somewhere? It's like... it's like we knew each other before? In another life, maybe? You know, like in another universe – or something?" I said, as I began to feel slightly dizzy and almost to the point of passing out.

"Olivia, are you alright?" Asked Aiyana, as she began to walk over to me.

"Yeah, I'm fine! But I... I just need to know: who are you both?" I asked again – as I struggled to maintain my balance and my consciousness.

"Like I said, we're just visiting for a couple of days – that's all! I'm Mark, and this is my wife, Melissa – and we are here in the New Forest to do some walking, and some looking around, before we need to head back home. And tomorrow, while we are down here, we're going to the book-signing of a fellow author!" Said Mark with an intriguing smile.

"You? You're an author?" I asked, as I felt almost out of breath.

"Yes, I am! I've published a few books – mostly poetry, but I am slowly moving into short-stories. And, someday, maybe even novel-length stories?" Said Mark with a look of pride on his face, as he reached out his right-hand to his wife.

"And you are here to attend a book-signing, you said?" Asked Aiyana.

"Uh-huh, we're going to get some books signed by the mysterious and enigmatic author known as Vega! That is, we will if *they* actually show up to *their* book-signing? They are notorious for arranging these book-signings – and then not showing up! But, a week ago, they put up this cryptic message on their website saying that they were releasing this super-secret new book at midnight, the day after tomorrow? And they told everybody that they would actually be at this used-bookstore, called "The Crimson Bookshelf", on Venice Street, at 9 a.m. on the morning of their new book's release. But, to be honest, both Melissa and I are more than a little skeptical that Vega will actually be there? Because, like I said, they have never shown up to any book-signing before! And I don't think that this one will be any different? But, we will still be there to see if they actually make an appearance!" Said Mark with a smile. Mark Hastings – whose face, whose name, and whose voice, was all that I remembered seeing and hearing moments before I lost consciousness, and I apparently passed-out onto the forest floor.

Chapter Twenty-Four:
"I'll be there"

Two days after I fainted in the forest… two days after I woke up in my own bed again, as if I had just woken up from a dream. Two days after I looked up into Aiyana's eyes, as she stood over me with a cup of hot tea in her hands, and she told me about what had happened in the forest: about how she and Melissa had to physically carry me back to the cottage, and make Mark and Melissa – the couple who we had encountered in the forest – believe that I had fainted because I had low blood-sugar, which for all I knew could have been the actual cause? Because, to this day, I still do not know why I passed out like I did? Although, I do have my suspicions about the cause? And at the top of my list of suspicions, at the time, was that author that we met – *Mark Hastings* – who I thought might have be the cause, somehow? But, of course, I couldn't prove it.

I knew that both Aiyana and Melissa were worried about me, and that they were concerned about what my loss of consciousness meant and who or what was responsible? But I assured them that they didn't have to worry, because: *"It was probably just low blood-sugar?"* I told them.

It had been two days since I had heard Vega's name spoken aloud by another person – by another fan of his books – who had informed me that Vega was going to be having a book-signing of their new book that nobody had heard anything about – including me, and I had shared a bed with him for an entire week not so long ago?

And that day – when a great many of Vega's fans would be showing up to another bookstore, anticipating to actually see him, but who would leave disappointed because he was not going to show up – was today. And knowing that he would not be at that book-signing was the reason that I decided that I might actually go to that non-book-signing book-signing – not because I didn't want Vega to be there, and not because I didn't want to see him…

it was just that I didn't want to see him yet, and not until I was ready to see him again.

It had been just over a week since I had last seen Vega's handsome face, in person that is – however, in my dreams, on the other-hand, I had seen him over and over again, every night without fail.

It was 7 a.m. – 2 hours before the book-signing that Vega had arranged – and I was standing in the kitchen of Aiyana's cottage, as I looked out of the window, and I debated whether or not I should go to *The Crimson Bookshelf?*

Because who was I really going for? For myself? For Vega? For Vega's new book – which I could just as easily purchase online and have delivered to my door?

I didn't need to go – I kept telling myself. However, in my heart I knew that I did.

It was 8 a.m. when Aiyana came out of her bedroom and she joined me in the kitchen.

"You ok?" Asked Aiyana immediately, as she looked at me and then simultaneously turned on the electric kettle to boil herself some hot water.

"I... I... I don't know, if I'm being honest?" I said, as I looked at her for a moment and then I returned to staring out of the window.

"Want to talk about it?" Asked Aiyana, as she picked up her teacup from the kitchen sink.

"Not... Not really!" I replied – reticent to tell Aiyana what and who was on my mind.

"Huh? Yeah, I thought you'd say that! I must be psychic, huh?" Said Aiyana with a smile, as she continued to retrieve the sugar and the milk that she would need to make herself a cup of tea when the electric kettle had finished boiling the water.

"Maybe you are? It's certainly not out of the realms of possibility?" I said with a smile, intending only to be humorous.

"True! Very true!" Replied Aiyana, playfully. "So, you been up long?" She asked, as the water from the electric kettle started to boil.

"Not long!" I replied.

166

"You? You got plans today?" Asked Aiyana – as she started to put the sugar and the milk into her teacup, followed soon after by a teabag and some boiling water from the kettle.

"Why?" I asked without hesitation.

"No reason! I'm asking just in case you needed to use the car? It's just that I might need to head into town in a little while? And, if you need to go too – maybe I can give you a lift? Or, if you need it, you could use the car instead? And I could just as easily walk?" Said Aiyana with a smile – as she stirred the milk, the sugar, and the teabag, in order to make herself her cup of tea to her liking.

"I... I... I don't know?" – was all that I could say in reply; however, on the inside, I could hear the Wolf wanting to make its voice be heard.

"Well, why don't I just take the car for now? And then you can use it later? How about that?" Asked Aiyana – my response to which almost brought about a panic-attack from within me.

And over the next few seconds, I took a deep-breath and I asked myself what I wanted to do? However, I knew that I did not have long to decide whether I was going to go to Vega's non-book-signing book-signing, or not? Because time was quickly ticking away.

"I... I..." I started to reply – but, for some reason, I couldn't make the words that I wanted to say come out of my mouth?

Then I saw Aiyana go over to the sideboard cupboard unit in the living room, and pick up the keys to her old Land Rover that was parked outside the cottage – and it was at that moment when I found my voice again, and I said:

"Yes! Um, I... I might use the car actually, if... if that is ok with you?" I said with nervous urgency in my voice, as I walked over to where she was standing with her cup of tea in her right-hand and the keys to the Land Rover in her left-hand.

"Really?" Asked Aiyana with what looked like a look of intrigue on her face. "Okie dokey! I guess that you can use the car today, and perhaps I can use it tomorrow to run some errands? If that is ok with you?" Said Aiyana with a smile, as she gently handed me the keys to the Land Rover.

"Sure! Thanks! Thanks, Ana!" I said with a smile – as the prospect of me having a full-blown panic-attack diminished considerably.

"Not a problem!" Replied Aiyana. "So, you going to be heading out soon? I thought that I would make Missy some breakfast? You hungry?" Asked Aiyana, as she looked at the clock hanging on the wall of the kitchen – as did I.

"I... I... yeah, I... I'll probably be heading out soon, to be honest!" I replied, as I looked at the wall-clock and I noticed that it was almost 8.25. "So, I... I guess that I better get my things together? Thanks again, Ana!" I said with a smile, before I walked out of the living room, and then I made my way back to my bedroom – where I immediately started to prepare the satchel that I carried almost everywhere... and the same one that Vega had given me a long time ago.

Soon after, I said goodbye to Aiyana and Melissa both – and then I left the cottage, I jumped into the drivers-seat of Aiyana's old Land Rover, and I drove into town.

●

I waited outside *The Crimson Bookshelf* – in line and along with many other fans of Vega's books – in the freezing cold, as I and everybody there waited with bated breath for the doors of the bookstore to open and for Vega to, hopefully, be waiting on the other side for us to come in.

Some fans must have been waiting outside all night and all morning – because their lips were blue, their faces were red, and I could tell that they were just talking just to keep their minds off of the cold weather that they were having to endure just so that they could potentially meet their favourite author? And I absolutely understood their passion and their reasons for doing what they were doing – but I also knew that Vega was not going to show up.

And I wasn't wrong: because when the doors of the bookstore finally opened, and every one of his fans that had been standing in-line started to rush in, as if they were here to meet a rock star or something, He – Vega – was nowhere to be seen.

There were, however, multiple copies of his new book *"The Vampire and The Rose"* on display around the bookstore and stacked up for anybody and everybody to purchase.

All of Vega's fans who had shown up to this supposed book-signing were understandably a little disappointed – which could be heard in the wave of groans that some people expressed when they realized that Vega had not turned up, again; however, no true fan of Vega's was truly surprised by his no-show. Because this was what Vega did – and his fans had come to expect it from him? But his constant enigmatic antics did not dampen the passions, nor the love, that people felt for Vega and his amazing books. And it did not matter to anybody that they did not know definitively what sex Vega truly was – because they loved him just the same.

Of course, I was not surprised – however, I must admit, I was a little sad that he hadn't shown up. And when I picked up a copy of his new book, *"The Vampire and The Rose"*, I… well, I broke down in tears – quite frankly – as soon as I read what he had written on the dedication page:

To my Rose –
To me you will always be beautiful…

To my love –
I will always be in awe of
The Wolf in You

And I couldn't help myself: I started to cry almost immediately, because I knew that that dedication was meant for me… and I knew that even though Vega was not there in that bookstore, he was trying to tell me that he would always be with me and that he would always love me.

I was… I was speechless! I… I… I didn't know what to think? What to feel? Nor did I know what I should do next? Because all I wanted to do at that moment was to find Vega – wherever he was – and kiss him on the lips. But he was not there – and I had no idea where he was, nor if I would ever see him again?

I don't know how long I stood there in that bookstore, clutching onto Vega's new book – however, at some point, I guess the Wolf decided to wake me up from the daze that I had fallen into, and then I slowly went over to the cash-register and I bought the copy of *"The Vampire and The Rose"* that I was holding on to.

I drove home. I sat down on my bed. And then, I cried myself to sleep – not letting go of Vega's new book for a second.

Over the next three days, I spent every waking hour reading every word of every chapter of Vega's new book – not wanting to put it down until I reached the bitter end; however, when I did finally reach the end of his book, I discovered that Vega had ended his book – a love story between a Vampire king and the love of his life – with a happy ending, in which his couple lived happily ever after together.

I read the last chapter of *"The Vampire and The Rose"* over and over again – because, to me, it was an idealized version of a perfect ending to an amazing love story, and also because it was a complete juxtaposition to the story of Vega and I and how it had ended.

I wish that our story could have ended as happily as the vampire king and queen in Vega's new *Vampire Spirit* book – however, most love stories do not end as you would hope they would; but that is the thing about love: it is sometimes unexpected, unpredictable, unbelievable, unconventional… but, if it is meant to be, then love will overcome any and all obstacles in its path.

I had no idea if Vega would always love me – as he said he would; but I knew that I loved Vega, and at that moment I could not envision a time when I would not be in awe of him.

I was beginning to believe that I was the only reason that *"The Vampire and The Rose"* even existed, and that Vega had written it for me so that I would always know that what we shared meant something to him – just as what I knew we shared meant something to me. So, with that in mind, I decided to return the favour and do something for Vega.

I asked Melissa to help me find the journal that I remembered I used to write in – over 15 years ago, by that time – when I was staying in this cottage and being looked after by Tala – Aiyana's mother, and the controlling witch who had intended to use me for her own gains. Anyway, after a few hours of looking through all of the things that Tala had left behind before she died, and some of the things of mine that got left behind at the cottage when Melissa and I moved up north, packed away in a dusty cardboard box, we found it! The cardboard box that we found it inside of was old and looked to be on the verge of decomposing however, my old journal looked in the same condition as it had done 15 years before.

I had begun writing in my old journal just after I lost Terry. And, as I read through the journal entries that I had made at the time, I realized how much I still missed Terry. I even, quietly, wished that I had a time-machine – so that I could go back in time, and rewrite some of the events from the past, and make different choices to the ones I had made? And, of course, find a way to save Terry? However, then I began to feel guilty for thinking that way – because if I had not become the Wolf, for example, and if I had not gone camping with my friends all those years ago, then I may never have even met Terry? Nor would I have had Melissa? Nor would I have Aiyana in my life? And who knows what kind of boring and predictable life I would now be living?

I loved Melissa – to me, she was the best daughter in the world! I loved Aiyana – because, to me, she was the best friend anybody could ever wish to have! And, I loved The Wolf – because I would not be who I am without them... and because they are me, and I am them! And I felt incredibly blessed to have the gifts in my life who had been there for me when I needed them the most – and I loved our little unconventional family.

Like I said, I wanted to give something back to Vega in the same vein as he gave to me – so, after reading through my journal entries over again, I decided that I would write something for Vega.

I spent hours just looking at a blank white page in a notebook, just trying to figure out in my head what I wanted to write and what it should be called. I had a few ideas, and a few titles rattling around in my mind: "The Wolf and Me"? "The Vampire and Me"? "The Enduring Love"? And then another title came into my mind, and with it I knew exactly what I wanted to write about.

What about "The Wolf in You"? I thought to myself – and when I realized that that was going to be the working title of the story I was going to tell, everything started to come into focus.

So, I sat down on my bed – with my notebook in one hand, and with my silver pen in the other – and I began writing the first line of my story:

My name is Olivia Hunter... and I am a woman who is about to take a brand new leap into the unknown.

And that was the when, the where, the how, and the why I decided to tell the story in front of you, in collaboration with another author who you may have heard of – the true story of Vega and me, and the stories of *The Wolf in Me* and *The Wolf in You*.

THE END

Mark Hastings is an author from the United Kingdom.

He is a passionate poet and storyteller who loves sharing the inspiration of his imagination, and transporting people to other worlds.
He loves writing, reading, listening to music, watching films and T.V. shows – but above all else he loves his family, his friends, and most importantly he loves his beautiful fiancé, Melissa, truly madly deeply.

Mark's books:

Poet of the Sphere

The Sound of Mark

The Eternal Boy

The Dreamer and the Dream

Truly Madly Deeply

Too Close To The Sun

The Wolf In Me

Playing God

Are available as eBooks or in Paperback at:

Amazon.com
Amazon.co.uk